fagih@hotmail.com

CHARLES, DIANA AND ME AND OTHER STORIES

Ten of Ahmed Fagih's best short stories are included in this memorable collection providing a reading experience that is both entertaining and socially relevant. Although focusing on contemporary themes such as the conflict between self and society, and the tension between conservative concepts and modern values, Fagih retains his signature style of writing. Always poetic, with a characteristic mixture of illusion and reality, the author brings to Western culture stories that have delighted Arabic audiences for years.

CHARLES, DIANA AND ME AND OTHER STORIES

TRANSLATED FROM THE ARABIC

AHMED FAGIH

KEGAN PAUL INTERNATIONAL
London and New York

First Published in 2000 by
Kegan Paul International Limited
UK: P.O. Box 256, London WC1B 3SW, England
Tel: 020 7580 5511   Fax: 020 7436 0899
E-mail: books@keganpaul.com
Internet: http://www.keganpaul.com
USA: 61 West 62nd Street, New York, NY 10023
Tel: (212) 459 0600   Fax: (212) 259 3678
Internet: http://www.columbia.edu/cu/cup

Distributed by

John Wiley & Sons
Southern Cross Trading Estate
1 Oldlands Way, Bognor Regis
West Sussex, PO22 9SA, England
Tel: (01243) 779 777   Fax: (01243) 820 250
E-mail: cs-books@wiley.co.uk

Columbia University Press
61 West 62nd Street, New York, NY 10023
Tel: (212) 459 0600   Fax: (212) 259 3678
Internet: http://www.columbia.edu/cu/cup

ISBN: 0-7103-0631-8

British Library Cataloguing in Publication Data
Applied For

Library of Congress Cataloging-in-Publication Data
Applied For

Since the principal story in this book was written and published in Arabic long before the tragic death of Princess Diana, and since I can not now alter the events of the story, I thought of no better person or cause to dedicate this book to, than the cherished memory of the late princess.

Charles, Diana and Me and Other Stories

Contents

1

Charles, Diana and Me

My remote, voiceless relationship with Prince Charles dates back to when the Prince placed the engagement ring on Lady Diana Spencer's finger. His extraordinary choice of this particular woman was what made me snap out of my isolation, read the papers and watch T.V. once again; the major portion of my time and interest was devoted to news of Prince Charles and his charming fiancée. The engagement made me discover that I had something in common with Prince Charles, which I will proceed to tell you without much ado. Years before Lady Diana was born, I came across a book of selected love poems; on its cover was a picture of a face of a young woman, exactly like that of the face of the young woman whom Prince Charles brought from an obscure world into the limelight. It was a simple black and white sketch, devoid of any embellishment, just black lines on white paper, portraying a face with joyful, glowing eyes, looking at a dreamy faraway place, full of innocence and a mixture of royal pride.

And so a dream world was created for me, weaved out of the love poems in the anthology, the drawing of the anonymous artist and aided by my early days of youth. It was a dream that developed and grew, as time went by, to take the form of a woman, lent, by my imagination, a voice, scent and colour; lent a life, motion and warmth all of its own. Her picture conjures sweet feminine insinuations, resonations and reverberations. Eventually, this woman comes to inhabit my heart and fill all its emptiness and I find myself madly and deeply in love with her. In my sleep and in my wakefulness I see no woman but her. And so from my early youth, I became enthralled by that simple, naïve drawing of the face of the yet to be born Diana. I could not, thereafter, disentangle myself from her for she became my whole life from that day onwards; a continuous quest for a woman like the one in the drawing.

I have met many women; sought to have affairs with some of them, but inevitably, they would come up against the picture of the perfect woman, the woman of the picture. My choice of a profession as a wandering reporter was only because it would allow me the opportunity to search for her in the different areas of the world, after I had failed to find her among the women of my own city. I roamed the globe far and wide. On many an occasion, I thought I saw her among a party crowd, or standing at one of the train stations, or yet again reading a book under the light of a faraway window. The bother and pains I endured to get close to her: I would wait for her at stations, observe her from opposite that window or frequent public places, so as to get a really good look, only to discover that it wasn't her, so I'd leave and start my quest anew, in other places and on new pavements.

Suddenly I was caught unawares to find that I was an old man and still a bachelor. All I reaped from my quest was pain and disappointment. I stopped following the course of the sun from East to West and wretchedly returned to my home. I got used to being a bachelor. It became a way of life with which I became contented. I could not change it; I'd realised that the dream woman, for whom I had gone in search of, will always remain locked in the realm of dreams and fancy.

Then came the sunrise of my life, re-kindling it with excitement: the moment when the face of Diana beamed from across the newspapers and T.V. screen proving to me that the dream woman had a faithful and near-like genius personification in real life. There she was, as I had seen her four decades ago, upon the cover of my poetry book. Watching her in the company of her fiancé, her walk, her smile, her words, I only saw what I had already seen in my imagination over the past forty years. Through all those years, I'd lived in the company of that smile, felt its sweetness on my tongue; saw those bewitching eyes in their star-like luminosity, made more dazzling by the rapid movement of the eye lashes. While, that nightingale voice was like dewy nectar quenching the thirst of my happiness. It is her. That nose, mouth, eyes, hair neck and ears; those fingers, arms, chest, waist and legs. All that luminosity and transparency. This velvety charisma, full of pride, all that innocence that belongs to heavenly creatures. Exactly as I'd cherished her in my memory. She'd inhabited me all those long years of my life, with the selfsame features, once drawn by a genius of an artist, to suit my heart's desire.

True, she has come forty years too late, but I don't regret it. In fact, I'm glad she's here at long last and I thank God for that, for now I know for certain that my dream was not an insanity or an illusion. I am thankful for that handsome Prince because he's found her, and that fate should will it that our taste be the same; and our sense of beauty too. That he should choose what my heart has chosen. Undoubtedly, being a Prince, blessed with the people's love and having everything to live for, has made him much luckier that I in finding this girl that I had searched for all my entire life, in vain. To him I owe a lot of gratitude and thankfulness.

And so began my relationship with the Prince, whom I'd considered a kindred brother. I, also, started to follow his news and read everything about him, never letting up even when I was in my home country which is far removed from his. I traced the developing relationship between him and his fiancée. Their stupendous wedding day was a feast day for me. I made sure I attended it in London. I even took a room in a hotel opposite the palace in order to be close to the scene of events. Joyfully I took to the streets, dancing and singing with the people, exchanging toasts and watching the royal, bridal carriage. Then I was off to my room to see the televised wedding ceremony, live from St. Paul's cathedral to witness the actual moment of the happy union. When I heard that the Prince and Princess would come out onto the balcony to wave to the crowd, I was out on the streets again standing in front of Buckingham Palace, where I mingled with the crowd, looking up at the high balcony in a state of pure ecstasy and bewilderment, at the dream that was becoming a reality right before my very eyes, at the Princess who'd emerged from the palace of legends, and there, standing right beside her, is her Prince in full royal splendour; both waving at the crowd.

I made my way, shoving and pushing through the crowd to get a good position and have a really good look up close. I stood feasting my eyes on the scene before me, where reality fused with the imagination. I conjured a picture of myself, when I was the Prince's age. Oh! How I wished he'd take her in his arms and kiss her. Now, that would really be a first in royal weddings! I was, nevertheless, induced by an overwhelming desire to ask Prince Charles, my kindred brother, to do this unconventional thing for me and kiss her right there and then, to complete my happiness. To my utter amazement and without much ado or any hesitation, the Prince granted me my wish; he wrapped his arms around the Princess's waist, bent his face over hers, the Princess raised her beautiful mouth to meet his and then came the kiss, transmitted to the four corners of the world by the lens of the cameramen. At that present moment, I felt that the Prince's happiness was my happiness and that my relationship with him – the result of this spiritual communion between us and which had just undergone its greatest test – had been sealed with the stamp of sincere good will, thus rendering it a relationship of fate and destiny.

Getting to know the Prince's opinions and thoughts on public issues, I discovered an eerie affinity between his thoughts and mine. Moreover, I discovered that what he had to say about modern architecture and about maintaining the beauty of the countryside, as well as his talk on museums and books, all lent voice and meaning, form and content to all those equivocal feelings which I'd never really cared to look into before, or even given the chance to become complete thoughts, not that is, before I'd heard him talk. It was as if he were talking on my behalf. Whenever I hear him speak so eloquently, in that deep, sincere and warm voice, I feel so proud of this similarity between us. Sometimes, I would even mutter some form of encouragement such as 'Well said Charles!' or then again, 'That's right give it to them.'

One evening, as I was watching a live televised event on telly, I was so angered by earlier newspaper reports that had criticised the Prince for interfering in matters of government, so much so, that I found myself telling him before he began his speech:

'Please don't let me down. Don't give in to their blackmail. Tell them in no uncertain terms that if they want to restrain you this way so as to do absolutely nothing, then you'd rather leave this country for good.'

It came as no surprise to me, when the Prince headed towards the rostrum and repeated exactly the same words that I'd asked him to. I was not surprised, because this communion between us was no longer a matter of astonishment or bewilderment.

Right at the very centre of the Prince's activities, which now captured all my attention, was his relationship with Princess Diana. Motivated by feelings of love and joy, I traced their blissful marital relation and the love and attention of the general public which enveloped them. How jubilant I was and lucky to live in this age of media revolution, which did all in its power to monitor their lives so intricately and closely, in turn enabling me to get to know everything about them, as if I was living with them, day in, day out. Being the royal couple that they were, soon to sit on the throne, they must obviously want their home to resound with the clatter and bustle of their heirs. I was happy because they were happy, because they had a wonderful marriage, and because they'd been blessed, twice, with two children to complete the portrait of a happy, royal family.

Something about Princess Diana, which I caught from my incessant observation and unending interest in the lives of the Prince and Princess, began to worry me. That youthful angelic faced girl, brimming with vitality, with eyes always downcast in a show of

4

coyness and timidity, was maturing, and, there was an ever so slight change in her countenance, possibly attributable to age and experience. That youthful girl had become more forward in her address to strangers, her eye lashes had become steadier and her infinitely dreamy eyes had become more knowledgeable of her wants. I was well aware of the shortcoming of my outlook, springing as it did from a steady and unchangeable vision of my dream woman, more akin to that of a photo of a dear friend in the album of memories. That is probably why I was weary and cautious of any change in the picture of my dreams. I was simply trying to reconcile between what life presented in reality and between the image engraved on the walls of my memory. How can one retain the freshness, modesty and paradisiacal innocence of the eyes of the woman of one's dream, despite the tricks of time?

I got worried at what I saw, the more so, because I was afraid that this feeling I had would communicate itself to Prince Charles. I wanted to spare him that. I wanted him to be more positive and conscious of the seriousness of these thoughts of mine which were, in the main, due to my mental state, reflecting my sense of betrayal inflicted upon me by the continuous and rapid movement of time. But what can I do about this open, spiritual communion between us. For his sake I must try to master my emotions, so as not to be unfair to a love that has grown and developed under my care.

Whenever I read that she'd sacked palace staff or heard about how she'd made a cruel remark, I would tell myself this could never be, for it's not in keeping with the innocence and transparency of the woman I knew, even before her birth. I could even go further and say that such behaviour does not come out of the naïve beauty for which my dream woman is characterised. Her roundish face became less and less so; it became more longish in feature, I would explain it away to myself as a result of her pregnancy. But when that was over and still her babyish, roundish face did not return, I would believe that was because she was now Diana the wife, the mother and the Princess with public responsibilities.

For the first time since I'd seen her picture over the cover of the selected poetry book, my feelings for her became tepid, if not downright cold. I was somewhat saddened, because this woman had been the focal point of my entire life. What a high price to pay, but I did so willingly and happily, even when I looked at myself and at my friends to find that they were blessed with the warmth generated from having a family and children while I was all alone, because I did not want to let down a girl, whose picture was tatooed and fire branded in my memory and by the same measure I did not want her to let me down. Nor do I want the woman who'd borrowed her features to develop and grow in a direction contrary to my heart's desire.

My worst fears were confirmed when I glimpsed flashes of her angry moods on T.V: taut nerves, swaying moods, these were all characteristics that were not part of the spirit and manners of the woman who had polarised my emotions for all my life. This new irritable side of her personality, which is completely contrary to her former self, was the sad and woeful cue for shattering my whole dream.

But what about the man who saw this woman through my eyes, who'd chosen her with my heart. Has he connected with my crisis so as to become his own personal crisis. Has he discovered as I did that this woman is no longer the same woman that he'd married!

It was only natural thereafter, that I would be among the first to believe the news about differences between them. The tabloids vied among themselves to be the first to report about these differences, while other newspapers denied the reports, so did the Prince and Princess. But I was absolutely certain that a split had occurred. I was in no doubt that my expectations had come true. All my feelings of pain and bitterness were transferred from my weary chest by spiritual carrier pigeons into the Prince's chest.

I was fully responsible for what had transpired. I know for certain that this dispute should never have occurred. The Prince's love would never have changed from his wife were I not so profuse and extreme in my emotions. A prisoner of an obstinate psychological state, which had so exaggerated its depiction of the change in the nature and manners of the Princess. I am destroying a marriage that is of concern not only to its partners, but also to millions of people; men and women who were fond of the couple and took them as their example in life. In my self reproachment I would tell her that, if I'd only budged a bit in my preconceptions, if I'd only gone along with time and sought to respond to the laws of change and evolution I would have come up with a solution to this problem. The Princess is not to be blamed because she is human like all the rest of us, susceptible to change as she gets older. She is still extremely beautiful, of supple figure and spirits. So why do I retain that picture of her on the cover of the book and refuse to see the new colours that have further enhanced the luminosity of the image. I was certain that if such an attempt had been made and succeeded, I would've saved the marriage from its inevitable sad end.

6

I spent many a day afterwards doing nothing but following news reports, going through recent pictures of the Princess and watching tapes of her activities and trips, in order to get close to this new image of the Princess. In desperation and with all of my heart and mind I sought to comprehend and understand the Princess, including her fits of anger, her independent personality, her bold looks and gestures, the way she stands and the way she sits. On several occasions I'd thought I had achieved a connection and interaction with her new personality and that all my being was receptive to accepting her and dealing with her as my dream woman, who had dressed in a more colourful outfit. But what can I do about those tabloids that know nothing of my dilemma and that are of no help at all. They're always giving out distorted information tearing up the new and old image of the Princess. They went so far as to claim she'd once attempted suicide, while giving sly insinuations that these changes were not something out of the ordinary, but that they were an original fabric of her character; a part that had lain dormant only to erupt to the surface with her womanly maturity and development.

I refuse to believe it, because if I do that would mean that I have given up on my dream and with my own hands wrought destruction of my fantasy. That is why I let them be and I go back to my own original sources: to the Princess Diana as she is shown on the screen to get at the truth. But my sight lets me down too and my eyes refuse to see the Princess, with the rumours and stories going about her. I see her in terms of contradictions: simple yet complex, violent yet innocent, a dust laden star, a sun pursued by darkness, a royal flower overwhelmed by a snowstorm, blowing out the torch of love that had lit up the darkness of my heart. I'm in a jam, I don't feel well, I'm incapable of understanding or digesting what has happened. There is something in this world, something cruel and vulgar which is preventing the lark of happiness from singing forever, that is preventing the blossom of love from giving out its fragrance for time eternity.

In a tense and frustrated moment, I throw away the papers and tapes, I close the T.V. and I decide to wash my hands of the whole matter.

I realise that by doing so I have reached the end of the road and that I am forced to condemn this relationship to its calamitous end : separation. I realise that I will bear the heavy burdens of my sins for the rest of my life, because I have failed to save this love from destruction.

7

Forgive me, O friend Charles.

Forgive me O beautiful Princess, whose old image is still engraved on the walls of my heart.

2

A Story from the Babies' Ward

The nurse brought him into the ward for newly-born babies, laid him carefully in the cot; he was crying so she put the feeding bottle to his mouth. The baby stopped crying and pretended to be busy with the bottle. At the same time he was watching her out of the corner of his eye. The nurse left the ward and he gave a sigh of relief as if she had been a mountain weighing heavy on his chest. He threw the feeding bottle through the window, jumped lightly out of the cot and went strolling round the ward to make the acquaintance of his little colleagues, also just born. He visited them one by one in their cots, shaking hands and congratulating them on their safe arrival. It was a happy surprise for him to discover that at the Maternity hospital they did not mind promiscuity. Contrary to his information, they allowed boys and girls together in the same ward. He felt elated to know that a great number of the babies were of the opposite sex. He picked the most beautiful of the girls and set about making her acquaintance. She did not have a name. So he gave her one, saying 'Be Layla.' Then he gave himself a name saying 'I shall be your Majnoun.' He did not hesitate or wait to declare his love. Layla, the feeding bottle still in her mouth, asked if he had had any love affairs in his life. He swore that she was the first love of his life, that his past experiences had been no more than childish flirtations. She thereupon felt secure and soothed by his words, responded positively to his love by moving the feeding bottle from her mouth and kissing him on the forehead.

He thanked her for this gesture and confided to her that this ward filled his soul with anxiety and depression. He suggested that they go to a poetic place more suitable for little lovers like them, and leave this one which was so lacking in any romantic sense. She hesitated for a while, telling him that there were some ignorant and stubborn men in her family, that her father was living centuries behind the times, that his mentality was so rigid that he could not recognise the principle of women's liberation and objected to their going out without wearing a veil or meeting with the ones they loved. She warned him that to go out with him would be an adventure with goodness-knows-what consequences. The few-minutes-old baby was about to give up and approach another as his

9

beloved when Layla changed her mind and told him that she would risk everything for his love. He took her hand in his and together they jumped out of the window and ran through the back streets away from the hospital. They stopped at a deserted corner to catch their breath and to decide on the best place to go.

The problem was that they did not know anything about the town, as it was their first day of life. They must think of some means of finding a quiet spot where they could spend a nice evening out before going back to the babies' ward, late at night. She suggested that they buy a newspaper to get the evening's programmes, places of amusement where they could enjoy themselves. He liked the idea and went running to the nearest kiosk. They started to leaf through the pages, looking for a Readers' Guide. The paper, however, did not carry anything of that sort but to make sure he looked again. It was amazing. Where did the people of Tripoli go in their leisure time? All the advertisement columns talked about people changing their ages, or their names, listed congratulations, condolences, hundreds of business transactions, and tenders, tenders and more tenders. Where did people go then?

Layla was afraid, and the paper discouraged her even more. She thought it would be wise for them to hasten back to the babies' ward and the feeding bottle. There was no indication of any leisure place in this town, where they could enjoy love and life. But her little lover gave her no further time for hesitation. He saw a café not far away, took her by the hand and led her there. As soon as they sat down the waiters stopped work, the customers left their seats, and gathered round them, watching with astonishment. They were not accustomed to seeing a male and a female coming into a café so they hurried to view such a scene. A large mob, growing bigger every minute, encircled them. The two little lovers were alarmed, terrified, not knowing of any reason why the mob should flock around them, their eyes round as coffee cups, and hold them in a state of siege. The only way out was to flee. The baby took his Layla by the hand, they sneaked between the people's feet, and started to run away from the mob. Then they started looking at one another in amazement, still not knowing any reason for what was happening. With a quavering voice, Layla said :

'What if my father should hear about this?'

'Supposing he does hear?'

'He would kill me, you idiot!'

She asked him to take her back to the ward, to forget about illusions of love at such an early age, and to wait until she finished the bottle-feeding stage and started to go to kindergarten where he could meet her at the gate. This she thought would be safer. But he implored her to be more patient and more courageous. He promised to buy a car as soon as possible, so that they could go out together in it.

It happened that a man and woman were passing by, so he suggested that they follow them, as they surely knew a place to go and enjoy themselves. Before long they found themselves in a market. What a disappointment! So the market must be where people came to relax and spend their leisure. But what to do? They saw a television in one of the shop windows. It was showing a play about love, about a man and a woman who were experiencing a thrilling romance. They felt happy, their two little hearts full of contentment. Love, then, was still thriving in this town. The broadcasting station was celebrating it and showing it to the people. The play was followed by a religious man whose face gave an impression of piety, virtue and straightforwardness. Clasping their hands, they listened with love and tenderness to this reverend man. What a great sign of society's progress it was! What a marvellous, harmonious combination on the little screen, a talk on religion and a play about love!

But as soon as he saw them, the religious one flamed with anger; he started to shout at them and call them the ugliest names. He reached out his hand from the little screen, trying to throttle them. He saw in their coming to the market hand in hand an act of intransigence against religion and morals, an obscenity and a baseness. He spat on them and when they wiped their faces he went on to shout for help from the police, the fire brigade, ambulancemen and traffic wardens, all to come with their cars and motorbikes, to collect this 'vice' that walked the streets.

The baby boy was crying continuously. As for the baby girl she was terror-stricken and calling for her mother. She ran off. The baby boy, following, took her hand and dragged her out of the market, and they raced along until they reached the Maternity hospital.

By now, news of the scandal had travelled there. The families of both babies had already washed their hands of them and refused to acknowledge them. The head of the hospital called for a staff meeting to think of a way out of the crisis, and how to get rid of these two renegade children. After an hour's deliberation, the hospital management decided to pass the case to the Grand Mufti, who has the supreme authority to make them go back to the place where they came from; nothingness.

11

3

The Stars have Disappeared, So Where are You?

The words of a folk song he used to sing a long time ago with his drinking companions on their outings to the outskirts of the city came back to him. The words spoke of the stars which disappeared and the sweetheart who arranged to meet her lover, but failed to show up. He was pleased at remembering the song and began to hum the tune, discovering just then that he had a talent for singing and that his voice had a good quality which only dawned on him at this very moment.

He had just consumed a couple of drinks with a friend who lived in this suburb. Whenever his friend had acquired some wine, he would invite him over to share the drink. His own house was not very far off and the full moon was almost as bright as the sun. Also because driving under the influence of drink is a risky enterprise, he decided to leave his car parked in front of his friend's house and walk the short distance home.

His path led across an open patch of waste ground. He immediately began to imagine that this space was the vast dance hall of a monarch who ruled over half the world. An uncontrollable urge to dance overcomes the king and he thinks that surely now, in the absence of the guards and the court entourage, he can enjoy this privacy and relax a little from restrictive ceremonies and rigid protocol. So why not dance with the reckless abandon and frenzy of a demon; or leap up into the air like a child; or play hopscotch; or balance on his hands instead of walking on his feet! He spread his arms out to his sides and sang, whirling around himself rapidly until he almost collapsed dizzily on the ground. He felt a child-like happiness take possession of his whole being and was not embarrassed to laugh out loud. Soon he discovered that the moon stood directly overhead and a royal whim to touch it overcame him. He jumped up as far as he could but failed in his attempt, so he gave up the idea as the passing fancy of a monarch. He proceeded to cross the waste ground in dance-like steps, endeavouring to match them with the tempo of the song he was singing:

'The stars have disappeared, so where are you? Oh... where are you?'

To his great surprise he was suddenly aware that a woman was standing near him. She had no doubt crept stealthily into the royal hall, and her provocative laughter echoed in the depth of the night, tinkling like a bell. She was probably the queen, arriving just to spoil the pleasure of his temporary solitude. It quickly dawned on him that this was no mere figment of the imagination nor a game. It was in fact a real woman, standing nearby, laughing at him in a loose and wanton manner. The wine fumes quickly evaporated from his head. She had probably seen him leaping into the air like a maniac, spinning around himself and laughing like an idiot! He stood rooted to the spot, his throat turned as dry as wood and he was unable to sing any more. He felt embarrassment descend upon him like ice and he begged God to turn him into a rat! But before being transformed into such a creature, he heard the woman calling him.

He wondered where on earth did this licentious woman spring up from at this hour of night? Her voice was soft, ultra feminine, insistently calling his name in the tones of someone boldly and shamelessly inviting him to a secluded spot to indulge in an indecent act. He looked in astonishment in the direction of the voice but could see no one there. He fearfully twisted his head to the right and to the left, he looked behind him and in front of him but there was nothing at all to be seen!

He felt death in the form of liquid tar start to seep up his legs. The woman's voice sounded very clear and close by, a hoarse whisper, full of coyness, seduction and sexuality. He could not pinpoint its origin, but it was only a few paces away. He was able to discern the shape of the buildings in the moonlight. He could see the stumps of felled tree trunks scattered here and there around the waste ground which used to be an orchard, but was now a piece of land sold for development. But there was still no trace of any living being anywhere. His house was some distance away and death continued to creep up like tar from his feet to his legs until it reached his knees, paralysing him. The woman's voice was still close. Exciting and terrifying it reached him in sound more like a hiss. She was calling him by his first name, enunciating it in ingenious ways and contriving to pamper and coddle him as if they were bound by old ties of intimacy.

She sounded impatient and demanding as if she had waited a long time for this moment. She had prepared herself for him and could find no better opportunity than this deserted spot, this night and this moonlight to meet him. He stood there unable even to cry out, looking up and down stupidly, not knowing whether the sound emerged from a hole in the ground or a hole in the sky! He remained stuck to his waist as the debauched voice started to get undressed. She brazenly removed her clothing, piece by piece, exposing a primordial body he could not see! She was suddenly overcome by lust, her voice growing even more insistent, almost like a howl. Fear gripped his heart, he wanted to scream, call for help or run away, but was unable to move or make a sound. He froze on the spot like a wax statue as the deadly tar continued to seep up his body, threatening to reach his throat. She continued to raise her voice, calling him unashamedly. He felt her breath on his face, her perfume filled his nostrils. Her vibrant body, burning with desire, sent out a hot blast which caused the sweat to pour from his neck.

The pitch of her voice began to acquire an indignant note, petulant and vexed. It was obvious that she was now trying a different approach. The queen who had spent an age in front of the mirror, combing her hair and completing her adornment and getting perfumed for his benefit, arriving on this bright moonlit night, stretching out her arms and presenting herself as a pure gift and a generous offering was now filled with indignation. She realised that the man she had chosen out of all others in the world, the man she was offering herself to, was reluctant to accept her invitation. Her voice became enraged and she started to roar out commands. It was no longer a dreamy look, two outstretched arms welcoming him eagerly and longingly. She no longer put her head to one side in a coquettish and coy gesture. The queen now stood erect and held her head up high, arrogant and proud, and proceeded to issue her royal commands.

He sensed the severity of the situation and wished he had the power to speak, cry or make a move. Perhaps he could kneel on the ground near her and swear by all that was holy that he was a supplicant at her court, and the only thing wrong was his inability to see her or discover her location. Still, the black tar encased his body so that he was not even able to breathe. He could not find the origin of the voice, nor was he able to see anyone around. The voice increased its passion and ferocity, threatening and menacing. A voice laden with violent royal fury, it was such that if he should hesitate to obey its command for one moment, a dreadful thing would happen. A hand, grasping a whip whose thongs had been soaked in brine, would soon emerge and lash him, ripping the skin off his face and back and killing him. A gun would suddenly materialise in front of his eyes and riddle his brow with bullets. A bomb would soon explode under his feet. She was now ordering him to her chamber in the ominous tone of someone who would flood the face of the earth, or rip the world asunder with thunder and earthquakes, or set the whole globe on fire, should he fail to go to her immediately and throw himself into her embrace!

He realised that he was surely doomed. The black tar had risen to his neck and was covering his mouth, nose, eyes, and forehead. He was now facing inevitable death, but before departing from the world entirely, the voice suddenly grew faint and distant. He quickly pulled his head out of the tar. He stood there watching and listening out for the voice in astonishment as it reached him faintly, weakly, afflicted by fatigue and exhaustion. Its commanding angry tones had disappeared. It was now broken, weary and far off – no longer an order or a threat, no longer coquettish or seductive. It had now turned into something like a cry for help, as if its owner was facing inevitable destruction. The voice reached him apprehensively, fearfully, crying and entreating rescue. It was as if she was all alone in the midst of a raging sea, surrounded by fierce and savage waves which threatened to engulf her. She was weakly appealing to the man's gallantry so he would rush to her aid. Her mouth was now filling with water, her calls for help were blowing bubbles in the air, and sounding like a gurgle. For some reason he felt that the voice, reaching him above the roar of the sea, was simultaneously very near, yet very far away. It sounded soft, waning, weakly imploring help. All traces of sexuality, seduction and femininity had disappeared from it.

Now that the voice had lost its menace, it sounded like that of a woman he had known. As he felt secure and had regained some control over his faculties, he could discern that it was familiar. He could not remember who the owner was, but he was certainly acquainted with the voice. It invoked in him old sorrows, as if he had spent a whole lifetime loving its owner, It was true that he had not yet experienced any emotional involvements, nor had any relationships with women. The only women he had encountered in his life, apart from his female relatives, was the prospective bride who was introduced to him one evening. But this was not her voice. Perhaps the woman was some mysterious being inhabiting his imagination! Or a woman who had frequented his dreams or it was the voice of a woman with whom he had exchanged a few words beh' ʼ ɪsed doors and which had stuck to his memory. It could one of the women he had known as a child, when he was ɔ attend women's gatherings without embarrassment and emained in his subconscious, until his song this evening

16

brought it alive. The feelings of dread had disappeared from his heart and were replaced by a genuine desire to save this woman from drowning. For a moment he imagined the open ground was indeed a sea and he attempted to close his eyes and plunge instantly into its waves, but the ground quickly returned to its former shape and the woman's voice, which was reduced to a gurgle, slowly faded away until it disappeared completely. He stood there bewildered and distracted. He felt worn out as if he had just run a distance of a hundred miles. As if he had suddenly grown old with ashen hair and trembling limbs. He was still rooted to the spot, but all traces of the fear he had experienced were completely gone. This feeling was replaced by one of deep sorrow and shame because he had stood by helplessly while the woman who loved him drowned. It seemed as if he had contrived and plotted against her with the sea. He tried to console himself with the thought that the phenomenon he had witnessed was a fantasy, or something akin to a nightmare. Perhaps it was the influence of a book on mythology he had read recently. Perhaps it was the wine, combined with the atmosphere of the deserted wilderness around him and the stillness of the night. All these factors may have contributed to the hallucination and to embodying all the disturbing thoughts that had gone through his head. Yet, how could this be plausible when he had been wide awake and heard her calling his name. Her voice still echoed through time and space. Her perfume still clung to his nostrils and he had felt her hot breath against his face only a few minutes ago. He was completely convinced that a woman who loved him had perished a short while ago as a result of treachery and betrayal. He had lacked the courage to respond to her invitation or to save her. She was without doubt the most beautiful woman in the city – captivating, seductive and enchanting – a most vibrant and potent woman. She had rebelled against the city traditions of segregation preventing men and women to mix and selected him from amongst all other men that night. She had decked herself in all her finery and put on her night attire. She had stood there, tall, exuding allure, her long black hair cascading around her shoulders like that of a gypsy. She had awaited his presence, her lips pouting and rounded deliciously as a ring and called out to him. She must have sensed the barrenness of his life and its emptiness; the harshness of the arid desert traditions in which he grew up. She wished to compensate him that night for his deprivation and descended upon him like rain on a parched life. No wonder she was rebuffed when the man she had presented with such an abundance of love had been unable to

17

succumb to her charms. Anger clouded her face like a fine sprinkling of freckles, thus increasing the loveliness and attractiveness of her features. She then threatened and promised dire punishment, but to no avail. She sensed that this was an omen of a failing in the universe and that an imminent disaster was about to overtake her. She cried out pitiously, imploring his help till the very end. He had stood by helplessly, he was useless, timid, burning with fever, his heart filled with terror, his hair turning grey, lacking in potency and courage. He was overcome by a sense of insignificance and self-contempt for being so ineffectual. Why on earth didn't she choose someone else, braver and more chivalrous? Someone more handsome, more daring and gallant who would have been willing to take the plunge into adventure? A courageous knight, not a deplorable timid mouse stuck in tar!

He suddenly remembered something. He was singing when she first appeared to him. The words of the song spoke of the stars which disappeared and the beloved who arranged to meet her lover but failed to turn up. Could she have been the lady of the song, arriving at the appointed hour and fulfilling the pledge she made to him? Perhaps she had heard his words and hurried to answer his request. She wished to refute the unjust allegations levelled against her of breaking her promise. She was attesting her sincerity, loyalty and honesty. She loved him, she wanted and desired him ... perhaps he was the scoundrel who could not keep an appointment or a promise? Was that the truth. Anyway, what was the use of such conjecture now? Everything was over. Whether what happened had been a dream or reality; whether the woman who met him in the moonlight was made of flesh and blood, or a wandering soul from another dimension; or a genie princess who left her father's palace to meet him – he was convinced – as convinced as he was that the earth rotated, that night followed day, that there was only one God and firmly believed with all his mind and heart that somewhere on his country's long shores a woman in the prime of youth and beauty had met death, by drowning a few moments ago. He had been stuck in tar and had failed to rescue her. He would definitely read in the morning papers the news of such a woman's death.

His whole body was convulsed with an uncontrollable urge to weep. He did not resist that urge.

4

The Wolves

The sky slept that night, closing all its eyes, not one star twinkled. The tree under which he sought shelter was old. Its ribs rose like those of a corpse which had died some years ago. Its aged gnarled trunk bore the burn marks of axe blows, dispersed with a sprinkling of several bullet holes. Perhaps some horseman had taken refuge behind it a long time ago to escape from a hail of bullets, just as he was now – a modern horseman – endeavouring to find some protection against the bullets of a cold winter storm.

His name was Othman Al Ghoul. He was no stranger to stormy nights. Ever since childhood, he had been shepherding goats, wearing only a long shirt, without a cloak, which the wind buffeted about, sometimes winning, sometimes losing.

This name was not given to him at birth, nor did he inherit it from his father or grandfather. It was a mark of distinction bestowed upon him like an honorary title or a medal being awarded to a war hero. He lived all his life like a ghoul whom people feared. He stole when the laws of hunger forced him to and killed when tribal battles compelled him to do so.

He lived away from people, escaping into the mountains and their rugged passes, untrodden by human feet. Even in the days when crimes of revenge flourished, the village had no one else to avenge it and protect it except Othman Al Ghoul. Many a song of rejoicing was heard in the village when Al Ghoul had successfully restored some plundered honour. Othman Al Ghoul acted as the cleansing agent for the village's dishonour. Even in disputes the challengers retreated in fear and left the land for Al Ghoul and his people to cultivate.

When peace had been established and crimes of revenge and plunder had been outlawed, Al Ghoul was loath to lead a settled life in the village. He searched throughout the wild mountain passes for a cave to live in on his own. He cut down trees to turn into fuel or collected halfa roots to sell. He existed like a lone old hyena moving amongst the mountains. He had a bushy black moustache whose ends twirled upwards. His complexion which was once an undetermined shade, had been transformed by long years of

19

exposure to the elements into a tanned hard countenance. When he appeared in front of people he struck them with awe and sent shivers down their spines. When he left the village that evening and returned to one of his abodes, the air was filled with clouds and dust. The sky had turned dark and the wind howled. The cold hid under cover of darkness and pounced upon him stealthily, pinching his nose and ears, and penetrated right through his tattered cloak to his entire body. He thought it wise to shelter by the old tree trunk against the stormy evil of that night, then resume his journey in the morning.

With roughened and calloused fingers, he gathered some twigs and chaff and built a fire. He warmed his hands over its flames and watched its smoke dissolve into the darkness. The darkness itself appeared no more than thick clouds of smoke. The storm raging around him was like a million howling wolves. The fire he built, his cloak, the tree trunk against which he rested, all retreated from the cold which was like a pitchfork stabbing his flesh. Othman Al Ghoul felt like a clay pitcher filled with icy water. The wind slapped and shook the branches and leaves overhead, which creaked and moaned aloud with pain, protesting woefully and desolately as if they were a mass of human beings getting crushed between the paws of a mythical monster. He removed a dry loaf of bread out of the folds of his cloak and placed it over the flames to warm and soften it a little, then set out to prove if his teeth were capable of chewing it.

Out of the darkness two approaching eyes glittered in the light of the flames, crawling slowly across the ground. They were not human eyes. They were small and slanting, in the midst of which two black pupils appeared like small old beads. A head then emerged with two ears. Little by little the rest of the body revealed itself. The approaching creature was a small grey wolf whose colour merged in with the surrounding darkness. Having regained its confidence, it seemed a friendly inoffensive animal. It lowered its head submissively and held its tail between its legs. It was a small hungry wolf whose bowels were being torn by hunger, causing it to venture forth out of its lair in search of food.

Othman Al Ghoul said to it:

'Let's share this loaf, little hungry wolf!'

The wolf squatted on its haunches some distance from the fire. It raised its head and pricked up its ears ... and waited.

Othman broke off a piece of bread and threw it towards it. Quietly and solemnly the wolf moved its head forward and picked up the morsel then swallowed it gratefully. It sat up waiting for another piece.

20

Othman threw another piece which the wolf caught in its mouth and gobbled it up quickly, then waited for yet another morsel. The wolf swallowed the pieces in silence and kept extending its grey head forward, its ears reflected the glow of the fire as it waited for more bread. Othman threw the last piece of the loaf which the wolf chewed quietly and remained in its place.

'It's time for you to go, you crafty mouse! I've given you my supper! What more do you want?'

He waved the edge of his cloak at it to chase it away. He shook his stick at it but the wolf did not budge.

He picked up a stone near him and threw it at the animal. The fur on its body quivered a little but it remained sitting there.

'What a stupid inconsiderate guest you are!'

The wolf began to annoy him. He picked up a glowing twig out of the fire and threw it at the wolf, catching it between the eyes and singing its forehead. The wolf leapt up in alarm, yelped and exposed its fangs in anger, then loped off into the darkness.

Othman sighed with relief. He knew how to get rid of that silly hungry wolf. He leant his head against the tree trunk, stretched his legs out and tucked the cloak closely around himself and settled down to sleep. Just before his eyelids began to get heavy, he heard the howling of a wolf somewhere nearby, issuing forth like a rocket. It was a prolonged bark like a cry for help. This was followed by a period of silence during which Othman Al Ghoul thought the matter had ended there. He attempted to return to sleep but the howling was renewed, this time coming from all directions. It wasn't just one wolf howling, but several ... a distant sound carried forth by the wind ... then another wave was heard quite near, sounding like the whistling of bullets in his ears. The place was filled with howling and when he strained his ears, he could hear the sound of the pack running towards him from all directions.

Othman Al Ghoul sprang up in alarm, his ears pricked apprehensively and realised that the wolves were plotting against him. The little wolf had cried for help. The other wolves in the vicinity had answered him and hurried in his direction. He knew these wolves. It happened once that a hungry wolf called out for the rest of the pack. In those days carrying firearms was permissible. He had fired a volley of bullets and scared them all away. This time, however, he was completely unarmed. What could he do to escape this trap? Soon a score of hungry wolves would attack him, sink their fangs into his body and devour his flesh and bones. He looked all around him. With emotion he realised for the first time that he wished he could glimpse even the shadow of another human being, or even a spark from another camp fire in the distance. This would have been enough to reassure him and encourage him to face the situation bravely. But there was nothing but the darkness and the storm in this desolate spot, cut off from the rest of the world. The night had erected black walls all around him. He was completely isolated. The world had emptied its vessel of all other human beings. No one was left except for himself and he must now face the wolves on his own.

The wolves began to converge, he could hear the tread of their paws approaching from behind one of the knolls. With an instinctive impulse for survival he refused to submit to instant defeat. He grasped the trunk of the terebinth tree and began to climb it hastily. When he reached the top he was able to see the wolves sniffing around the area as they swarmed around the embers of the fire. There were many in number, exceeding ten and they were all led by that little grey wolf who was not satisfied with eating his supper, but wanted to spill his blood and chew up his liver and lungs!

When the wolves discovered his location at the top of the tree they exchanged looks and growled. They all attacked the tree at once, attempting to climb it, and sink their claws and teeth into its old trunk. The storm too was conspiring against him. It mustered all its force of cold and wind to attack the branches of the tree and reduce him to a dry frozen twig. All that mattered to him was to find a strong branch not swayed about by the wind, on which to secure a firm foothold. When he managed to do so, the wolves had by then completely surrounded the tree. He broke off a branch with which to beat them off. The wolves had divided the task of dislodging him between them. Some set about digging the earth and scratching under the roots to loosen the tree after they had failed to climb it. Others stood up on their hind legs, and stretched their front legs, sinking their claws into the trunk in an attempt to get a better grip and climb it. Their howling mingled with the rumbling of thunder, the wind and the creaking of the tree. Al Ghoul's heart sank to his feet and his knees began to tremble with fatigue. He was panting heavily and breathed with difficulty like a strangled man. He felt that at any moment now, in the space of an eye blink he would fall off the tree and into the fangs of the wolves. He continued to wave the branch to the left and to the right, in front of him and behind him as the wolves leapt up into the air, almost reaching him. He wished the terebinth tree was a bit taller. He tried to move his feet onto a higher branch, but it broke under his weight. One of his feet almost slipped right into the gaping jaw of a wolf, which was trying its utmost to climb up towards him. This excited the animal which bared its fangs and leapt up even higher into the air. But with a superhuman strength he didn't know he possessed, Othman Al Ghoul pulled his foot out of the way before the wolf grasped it. His heart trembled with terror when a fork of lightning lit the sky and in that instant the eyes of the wolves glowed in its reflection. He saw several fierce hungry eyes and gaping jaws surrounding him on all sides. The wolves too saw him outlined clearly against the sky and set up a terrible howling which rang horribly in the depth of the night, echoing throughout the valley. It seemed as if the whole universe was filled with wolves. It wasn't just the cold which froze his bowels and caused his nose, ears and lips to swell up. His body was like the branches of that tree, shaking and shivering. The cold, however, was bearable in comparison with those ravenous eyes which glittered in the lightening, looking like the eyes of demons or giants which had risen up under cover of darkness to destroy him and rip his body to pieces.

He was alerted by a jaw which opened up wide, out of which rose fangs like nails, near him and trying to drag him off by a foot. The world contracted all around him. He had dropped the branch with which he was defending himself and there were no higher branches on to which he could climb. The fangs of the wolf were getting closer to his foot. He mustered all his strength and daring and lifted his foot high up, bringing it down with considerable force over the wolf's head, causing it to crash to the ground and yelp horribly, then it ran away from the tree. It growled in rage and leapt up high in to the air like a demon. If Al Ghoul had not been holding on firmly to one of the branches, he would have been dragged down by that wolf. The night itself was working against him as well. It seemed to grow longer and stretch into an eternity.

He tried to break off another branch from the middle of the tree with which to repel the wolves' attacks. He suddenly felt something take hold of him from behind and forcibly pull him down. He nearly lost his grip and fell off in terror, for he was certain that one of the wolves had succeeded in reaching him from behind. He let out a despairing scream which echoed all around. His fingers clenched around the nearest branch and he turned around to look behind him but there was no wolf fastened on to his back. He discovered that the tail of his cloak had been dangling down and that the wolves had taken hold of it with their teeth and paws, and were attacking it, he took it off and threw it down for them to tear to shreds. He remained perched on top of the tree, facing the attacks of the cold without a cloak, naked underneath his long shirt. He felt the cold as he had never experienced it before. It was like a million whips lashing his back, ribs, face, neck and legs. The wolves resumed their attacks after being distracted for a short while by tearing the cloak to pieces. The lightening struck again and the scores of evil hungry eyes glinted once more all around him. His terror increased when he glanced down and saw that the wolves had succeeded in digging tunnels under the tree, laying bare its roots. A number of them had carried on scratching and scrabbling all along the length of each root until they reached their origins. Othman Al Ghoul realised that he was doomed and that the wolves who had not yet managed to get him at the top of the tree, would soon be able to topple it. There was no escape left for him.

Othman Al Ghoul reflected on the attacks he himself had waged on others in the past, the crimes he had committed and how he settled disputes. How preferable it would have been if he ended up as the victim instead of the murderer. It would have been better if he had been shot in the head by a bullet rather than fall prey to the fangs of the wolves, which would enjoy eating him piece by piece. Was he spared all that time from the horrors of battles only to end up now as a tasty meal at the table of these ravenous wolves? As if that fate was not enough, the accursed cold had penetrated right through to his liver, heart and bowels and was chewing them up. Othman Al Ghoul felt faint and weak as he confronted the wolves, submissive as a lamb led to the slaughter.

Almost imperceptibly the darkness began to dissipate and a touch of dawn started to spread over the branches of the tree. The birds awakening and filling the air with their songs. The dew glistened on the green leaves, soft and moist. The wolves began to disperse one by one. A few remained still trying to dig up the roots, but as darkness was disappearing, they gave up the attempt and they too slunk off.

The last wolf to sneak off was the small grey one for whom he had relinquished his loaf and who alerted the rest of the pack.

The sun was shining as Othman Al Ghoul climbed wearily down the tree, in a state of almost total exhaustion. He tiredly surveyed the area. Everything about it indicated that a terrible battle had been witnessed by the night, which disappeared as stealthily as the wolves did. The whole tree trunk was peeled and pared. The old ribbed trunk which bore the scorch marks of axe cuts and bullet holes, was now laid bare and white like the skinned carcass of a slaughtered sheep. Broken twigs and leaves were scattered all over the ground. The base of the tree was turned into tunnels edged by mounds of earth, appearing like the dug graves of tall men. The roots which lay buried under the soil were stretched naked for long distances, totally exposed. Bits of rags lay everywhere which he recognised as the remains of his cloak. Othman Al Ghoul stood there like a dead tree, dry, veined and yellowed. His arms, hands and face were covered by scratches and cuts which he had sustained as he climbed the branches for safety. Yet the wolves who had besieged him all night long were unable to touch him ... not a single claw or tooth mark was on him.

Othman Al Ghoul trudged back to the village, trying to hide inside his torn shirt, nearly jumping out of his skin every time a dry twig snapped under his feet. He was trembling, his hands shook and even his moustache quivered. He felt that he did not entirely emerge unscathed from his encounter with the wolves. He knew that something in him was eaten up by wolves.

5

A Drink of Water

I saw him approaching from a distance at dusk – a shadow, now rising then falling upon the ground. Sometimes I saw all of him, at others only his head, sometimes he disappeared completely from sight.

I quickened my steps.

The clouds drifted overhead, crawling on their bellies, filling the vast space of the sky with a clamorous silence.

It struck me that if the man was proceeding in my direction, I had nothing to offer him. All the leaves of the wormwood bush around me had withered, even the rush broom trees under which we used to find some shade had turned into dry sticks. The earth was yellow, a sickly colour, yielding nothing, just as my feelings had turned yellow, promising nothing. The trees had all gone after people had chopped them down and turned them into fuel.

The man was getting nearer. It was clear that he was heading in my direction. I braced myself for a fight and moved my hand towards my shotgun to release the safety catch.

The harvest had now ended and I was on my way back home. We had gathered the ears of wheat into large heaps, we threshed them and scattered the chaff into the wind. We filled sacks with the wheat. I left the harvest with none of my own. The food and water I had consumed had been deducted from my wages. What remained was barely sufficient to keep my family for a few days.

The man was wearing a grey cloak, with a shotgun slung over his shoulder, its muzzle rising a few inches above his head.

He made a loud rustling noise as he approached, raising clouds of dust around his feet.

The sun was sickly yellow, sloping wearily towards the black hills we used to call 'The Negress' Breasts' ... a sickly sun and an ailing earth. I, too, felt sickly. I thought of crimes of revenge and of highway robbers. The man was walking towards me. When the shadow of his shotgun fell near my feet, my unease increased. His countenance was a dusty pale colour, like that of a desert fox. His features were hard, as if carved out of granite. He had a bushy moustache and his face was unshaven. His feet were clad in sandals, they were big, with protruding toes which reminded me of snakes' heads. He stood in front of me. He had a large frame with wide shoulders. His shadow fell near mine and loomed over it, then I knew why his feet were so big. Out of his eyes sprang a hundred talons and wings. He pounced on me with a cutting gaze, he squinted his eyes so tight that his face filled with wrinkles.

I thought to myself: 'You'll find me a difficult quarry!'

A few moments dragged by in silence. He studied my face as if searching for my identity, before speaking:

'Greetings.'

'Greetings to you too.'

I uttered these words sharply and guardedly, as if what I really meant was 'Curses on you!' I wondered what his next move would be. No doubt he would order me to take off my cloak or hand over the money in my possession as was the custom of brigands. Instead he suddenly asked:

'I wonder, friend, if you can spare me a drink of water?'

He asked me this in apologetic and sincere tones. All feelings of animosity towards him disappeared. For the first time I noticed that his lips were cracked like the parched earth. I felt ashamed for suspecting him of an evil motive, when all he wanted was a drink of water.

When I handed him the water gourd, he clasped it with both hands, closed his eyes and raised it to his lips. His Adam's apple rose and fell rapidly as he eagerly gulped the water, until he made me feel thirsty too. When he finished, he sighed with relief:

'Curses on this thirst … it nearly killed me!'

He walked alongside me. I was no longer fierce, but became pleasant and mild. It appeared to me that he could be a trusting travelling companion. I felt some vanity and pleasure at having saved him from dying of thirst.

I reached for my gun and locked the safety catch. I started chatting to him:

'What's your name, friend?'

'Abdullah.'

'We are all "Servants of God".'

'They call me "The Westerner".'

He was silent for a moment, then continued:

'But now they call me "The Easterner".'

I thought to myself that perhaps he had other names, some people like to be known by several names. Indeed even God himself is known by ninety nine names, which is fine … The man thought that the matter was still unclear to me, so he volunteered an explanation:

'I left my birthplace when I was young and travelled East ... I lived there for several years ... my name became "The Westerner" because I arrived from the West. When I returned to the West, people here started calling me "The Easterner." Perhaps I shall travel to the South and return, then people will call me "The Southerner" and so on until I am known by the names of the four corners of the earth!'

He laughed.

His laughter was pleasant and sincere, but also sad, like someone who had reached a compromise with his sorrow, and was able to live in harmony with it.

Despite the apparent pride in his voice, I sensed that the man had undergone a profound experience in his life which I resolved to respect. As we proceeded together down the road, he seemed to me like an old friend. I discovered in that instant that I was no longer a barren arid land, already green shoots of love and amity were sprouting in my heart.

Night-time arrived. His features blurred in the darkness and I could no longer distinguish them clearly. When his voice reached me from the midst of the darkness it sounded like belonging to a different person. He grew closer to me and I felt a great affection and tenderness towards him. This was strange for I did not usually respond to people so readily. Experience has taught me to be cautious and on my guard, but his voice which rang out in the depth of the night was amiable and refreshing like the night dew, softening and mellowing his harshness.

It was filled with such a glowing and effusive quality. It made me open my heart to him and I began to reproach myself. How could I have failed to discern the warmth and friendship in his voice from the start? No doubt his features which appeared so rough and cruel at first sight, had concealed the sincere expression in his voice. His words were like warm milk freshly squeezed from the udders of ewes.

I waited for "The Easterner" to tell me what he did for a living, but he didn't.

I asked him in a friendly way:

'What do you do these days, my friend?'

As if I had opened up old wounds which he kept hidden under his cloak, the man trembled with an angry reaction. His voice acquired a gruff pitch, which deprived it of its glowing and graceful qualities.

'As you can see. I am a man who belongs to no place. I have no name, sometimes I am known as "The Easterner" and sometimes as

"The Westerner." I have no profession. Sometimes I work as a shepherd, sometimes as a woodcutter, either cutting down palm trees or rush broom, or collecting brush wood which I carry across my shoulders. Sometimes I burn trunks for making coal, sometimes I pull out the roots of halfa grasses. Sometimes I hunt the ewes of gazelles and sell their meat at the market. I have worked at all these things. I have borne a lot of insults and hardships but, now I have rebelled against all of them.'

He was suddenly silent.

He left me hanging there in suspense with his silence.

I said nothing. I began to realise that "The Easterner" was suffering from something, that something had angered him. I felt sympathy and compassion for him. In fact I reproached myself for stirring up old wounds. I waited for him to resume talking, but a long while passed by without a word from him.

Next day we reached the crossroads. I had to take the road leading to my village, he had to continue on his way.

. I felt regret at being separated from this man, but I had a strong feeling that we would meet again some other time. I stretched out my hand to bid him farewell, but he wouldn't relinquish it, as if it pained him to keep something back from me:

'Do you really want to know, my friend, why I rebelled against all those silly things? Do you really want to know why I set out yesterday when we met? Do you really want to know?'

I said nothing, so he continued. In a rush of emotion, his words tumbled out, cutting like the edge of a sword:

'I have avenged myself. I am not such a nice man as you might think'... he revealed everything when he uttered his real name. 'I am Sultan' Sultan the thief, the murderer, the highwayman, the most notorious and dangerous man in that part of the country. I asked in amazement:

'Do you mean you are Sultan, the ...'

He said nothing, he just hung his head down as if apologising.

I imagined that I would feel a great shock which would change my feelings towards him. I should feel sorry for having saved the life of a highway man. I should ... but nothing like that happened. I wanted this to take place, but it seemed at that moment that my will was powerless to determine what was happening. I accepted all this as if it was a normal natural reaction. What he revealed would change nothing in our relationship. In spite of what I wanted to clarify to myself, that he would have tried to kill me too had it not been for the drink of water which saved his life and saved mine too;

30

despite all this I still retained my feelings of affection and great respect for him. I shall keep this memory, the memory of a highwayman to whom I opened up my heart one night, and never closed it again.

6

The Grinding Mill

'Tick tick ... tick tick ...tick tick ...'
The beat of the mill rose up in the still and tranquil atmosphere of the countryside in a fast, regular and monotonous rhythm, like the heartbeats of a healthy man, sound of body and soul and in full possession of his senses.

The mill knew no rest until night-time when darkness fell with its sorrows and stray dogs. Only then did its heart stop beating and its blades cease rotating. Its metal sinews no longer moved and it sank into a long, deep and delicious slumber. But during morning, noon and evening it rumbled on constantly, grinding corn and barley into flour, belching out black smoke like a furious wind. Perhaps it was directing its anger at all those people who continuously brought their loads here, piling their sacks which bulged with grain. All of them beat their sticks on the ground and stamped their feet, insistently demanding that their flour be ready that very same day.

'Tick tick ... tick tick ...tick tick ...'
All day long it whirred on ...
Turning grain into fine flour ...
While the village listened to its clamour ...
The owner of the mill, Abdul Mawla, laboured on. Exhaustion caused beads of perspiration to ooze from his forehead, neck and arms. Rivulets of sweat trickled down the forest of hair which grew on his chest, mingling with particles of dust which flew around the air of the windmill, the dust finally settling all over his body.

The inhabitants of the village daily absorbed the sounds of the mill. Their eardrums had grown accustomed to its noise and daily chatter, which commenced at sunrise and terminated at sunset. Whenever a mechanical failure occurred which caused a stoppage, everyone – old and young, men and women – was sure to miss its sound. Not only that but they all felt that things were not in order. This sensation never left them until the windmill's heart resumed beating. Many of them felt that this sound was a secret and incomprehensible language, through which the mill related an eternal and mysterious story. No one knew when it started or when it would end or what it meant; yet it was story close to their hearts and they derived great comfort from listening to it every morning.

The monotonous beats rose, announcing the location of the windmill which was situated amongst ten small shops. These stores constituted the entire commercial wealth of the village. Around them rose the short walls of the houses, some of which were sound and solid, others were dented and crumbling. Those built of mud turned a yellowish colour with age. Residents of some standing in the village built their houses with bricks and mortar, the walls were then plastered over.

Those latter walls usually turned into an unpleasant black like the colour of crows. This was caused by the children in the village who considered these walls as a treasure they had discovered for themselves, and had the right to dispose of them as they pleased. They held pieces of coal in their fingers and transformed the white surfaces into experiments in sketching, writing and graffiti.

Many times these walls represented the village's daily journal. Any events of significance were recorded right in the middle of such walls the very same day they occurred. Even the ballads and poems composed by Ma'touk bin Soudallah expressing his philosophical interpretation of events, or satirising political figures were recorded on them. For example, his poem ridiculing De Gaul's nose or Khruschev's bald head; also his poems lampooning the local government. All of these could be found etched the day they took place on the pages of this journal.

Apart from these, one could often find exchanges of opinion or heated arguments. A boy would write a rude insult against another in a child-like scrawl. The other child would wipe it out and, pressing his little body close to the wall and in the process getting his clothes soiled with coal stains, would then concentrate on scribbling or drawing.

The first child, happening to pass by that wall, would find awaiting him a new batch of fresh and appetising insults and swear words! It was a complete journal, no different from any newspaper anywhere in the world with its writers, poets and famous critics.

At the back of these buildings stretched the fields and orchards with their dry crops and dry trees. The palm trees stretched their heads towards the heavens as if imploring aid. The houses, distant and dispersed, appeared as if they had strayed away from the village.

When the hum of the windmill rose in the middle of the village : 'Tick tack ... tick tack ...tick tack ...' it sounded exactly like the throbbing beats of its own heart. In fact most of the activities in the village centred around the mill. Groups of people arrived here, carrying sacks filled with grain on their backs, these being their only means of livelihood. Caravans of camels travelled here and waited in the courtyard of the windmill. The camels squatted down and waited to transport the end product on the journey back.

'Tick tack ... tick tack ...tick tack ...'

The windmill sometimes ceased functioning for an hour or so during the day because of a mechanical failure which was quickly repaired by Abdul Mawla. However, when the windmill stopped working for a whole day, this invariably indicated that something serious had happened. The mill, in all its long history, had experienced only three such occasions. The villagers memorised these unusual incidents of failure by heart. Not only that but they went so far as to note each day such a failure occurred as a significant date marker with which to time events which took place during that period.

One person would ask another any one of the many questions which usually hovered on the lips of the villagers, such as when did his cow give birth to its calf? The answer would be prompt, dating the birth of the calf by the date of the stoppage of the windmill: 'It gave birth to the calf two days after the day the mill stopped for the second time!'

The enquirer would then go away, every cell in is body permeated with total comprehension and understanding, for no one failed to remember the date when the windmill stopped for the second time.

The circumstances under which the windmill stopped for a whole day were indeed important. The first time was when Abdul Mawla's father grew weary of sitting in a cold corner of his house and preferred to travel to heaven, so he departed this earth and moved nearer to his Maker.

The second occasion was when the village decided to go on a total strike in support of the Algerian revolution. The store owners closed up their shops, Abdul Mawla stopped the mill and they all marched in the streets, shaking their fists with anger and stamping their feet with rage. Their voices rose to hoarse cries of protest as they demanded death to the imperialists and the liberation of Algiers.

The third instance was when Abdul Mawla was forced to change the blades of the mill which were worn out with age and were not functioning properly. Many people complained about this and threatened to boycott his windmill and go back to using their old hand mills. The threats grew stronger in tone thus not affording Abdul Mawla the opportunity for further delay or postponement. He had no option but to order a new set of blades from the city. He had to stop the mill for a whole day while fitted the new blades on. The old ones lay in the courtyard in front of the mill with their ribs exposed. Often children seized the opportunity when Abdul Mawla was busy to dance and play around them. These were the reasons for the three occasions of stoppage.

Abdul Mawla, the owner of the windmill, was neither fat nor thin, not old nor young and always wore a long sash around his waist, which he wound on several times, thus creating many folds in it.

His arms were tattooed with illustrations of stars, birds, gazelles and a girl's face, her eyelids and eyebrows darkened with kohl. These jostled with several other designs tattooed in a dark green dye. A reason for so many tattoos may have been because his mother, who was a tattooist by profession, could find no other medium on which to practise and experiment with except her son, on whom she unleashed her creative spirit!

'Tick tack ... tick tack ...tick tack ...'

Abdul Mawla hardly ever left his windmill. He worked it and remained by its side, filling his ears with the ticking sounds. His sweat mingled with the dust of its flour, his nostrils breathed in the pervading sweet aroma of the grains as they turned into flour. Together with his saliva, he swallowed the special sentiments he had for the windmill. Flour dust often stuck in his throat, causing him to cough a great deal. He always carried a stick in his hand with which to tap the sides of the quern, where grains of corn sometimes got stuck in the corners of its metal spokes. He often gave vent to philosophical observations as he did so, his voice rising above the rumbling of the windmill so as to be overheard:

'These days nothing in the world works without the tap of a stick!'

'Tick tick ...'

'Why? Because in my opinion.this world is a treacherous place!'

'Tick tick ... Tick tick ...'

'The world, God protect us, is an ass!'

'Tick tick ... tick tick ...tick tick ...'

'Nothing works and no path is straight and narrow. Nobody discovers the right path except with the aid of a stick!'

Abdul Mawla always ended his pronouncements with a huge spit against the world and a cheer accompanied by loud coughing as he waved his stick in the air.

Abdul Mawla never rested. He often turned round and round and rotated with the mill, as if tied to it by invisible strings which caused him to rotate continuously until he disappeared with the momentum of the motion.

He would weigh the grains and place a sack or an empty basket at the funnel-like opening. The flour poured out from between the jaws of the stone quern. He would then go inside the small inner room which contained the machinery, to check and assure himself that all were in good working order.

He asked his son Sayeed, who was nineteen years of age and who helped his father run the windmill, to select grain from that sack or the next and pour some into the box ready for grinding. The choice of sack did not depend on a first-come-first-served basis, but on order of seniority and importance. It all depended on the answer to the question: 'Who is the owner of the sack?'

The first priority was always reserved for the police officer. Next came the turn of the civil administrator, followed by the Sheikh of the village. The fourth priority went to the nearest relatives, then distant relations, then friends and neighbours. Lastly came the turn of the other customers!

Abdul Mawla was often a target for waves of envy which washed over him from some of the villagers who resented him. They were annoyed because Abdul Mawla beat them a long time ago to this lucrative business which no doubt yielded a handsome profit. These waves rushed over him, advancing and receding in their ebb and flow, but they did not bother him in the least. On the contrary, he felt great pride and vanity as any other human being would, having achieved a great victory.

On that particular morning, the people in the village heard the mill murmur in several consecutive awesome beats ... then there was complete silence. They wondered what had happened this time. No doubt some mechanical failure had prevented it from whirring and relating its daily story, and waited for it to resume operating. Others decided to save time and went to find out for themselves what was wrong.

They hurried to the mill, those who arrived late found the owners of the shops already gathered there. They were surrounding Abdul Mawla and were bandaging his arm which was bleeding profusely. They tore strips of cloth from their garments to stem the spouting blood but the white cloth soon turned red. They kept on tearing more strips of cloth but these soon looked as if they had been dipped in a pool of blood. Many people moved forward and attempted to close the gaping wound with their hands, but the blood dyed their hands red and oozed between their fingers. They tied a tourniquet around his arm but that was useless too.

37

One of the men holding on shouted out at the spectators to go and fetch the male nurse who was doubtless immersed in a card game with Saleiman in the only coffee shop in the village. Others were asking Abdul Mawla how the motor hit him to cause such a deep cut. He answered them as his face turned dry, pinched and wrinkled like the skin of a squeezed lemon which had lain out in the sun for five days :

'It was the propellers of the small ventilation fan which hit my arm ... and ... and ...'

They understood that the cause was the swift-rotating propellers of the ventilation fan which formed part of the mechanism and apparatus of the mill situated in the small inner room. His sleeve got entangled in it and he was attempting to extricate it when the accident happened. He stopped the mill and went out to stem the flow of blood but the severed artery continued pumping it out. When he was finally carried to the first aid centre, the attendant spent every effort to close the wound but the blood had ceased pumping out of its own accord. All the blood contained in Abdul Mawla's veins had been exhausted.

The rather dim and inexperienced attendant was at a loss as what to do next. All he was able to do was send an express cable to the city, requesting an ambulance to transport the injured man to one of the city hospitals, at least to be given a blood transfusion. But the city was a long way away. An hour passed ... then two hours ... then three and still the ambulance had not yet arrived.

As time passed and the minutes ticked away, Abdul Mawla's face grew pallid and ghastly, until his complexion turned ashen in colour. His eyes began to lose their vitality and sparkle, as if they were made of clay. They were no longer able to convey sharp and clear images to him, everything around him blurred, shimmered and intermingled. Even the voices which crowded around his ears sounded as if all the people gathered there were speaking in an incomprehensible language, exactly like that of the windmill itself. He always sensed that the windmill was foretelling such a future disaster as had taken place that day.

Images began to tumble before his eyes, then twist and turn rapidly around just like the propellers of the fan which struck his arm. A small whirlpool began to form which swallowed his feet, then moved up his body and limbs until it reached his lungs. He gasped: 'I witness ... I witness ...' but never completed the words. His body quivered for an instant, his head lay to one side against his shoulder and he was suddenly still. He had breathed his last breath.

Abdul Mawla's face was like dust as were his arms, outstretched by his sides. Everything in his supine body which was soon to be placed into the earth was the colour of dust. No doubt it was the eagerness of dust ... for dust.

People were paralysed with shock. No one could believe that Abdul Mawla's end would be so quick and so simple, and from such an insignificant wound in his right forearm. When they had recovered from their shock, the weeping started.

Sayeed cried out in anguish as he threw himself over the body. Death had sneaked up on his father and tore his breath away with such amazing speed, just like the speed and beats of the mill as it shattered the silence of the village early each morning. The women gathered in Abdul Mawla's house, beating their breasts and pulling their hair and hugging each other.

People prayed over Abdul Mawla's body as they dug a grave for him and then covered him with earth. Sheikh Younis read verses from the Koran in his ponderous nasal voice. The mourners sprinkled water over his grave and over the other neighbouring graves, then departed.

The thing that preoccupied the villagers most was who would inherit the responsibility for the windmill. They were all of the opinion that Sayeed would sell the mill to one of the rich men in the village.

Some said that Sayeed would send it back to Tripoli. He would not be able to sell it here because no one was willing to buy a mill which could kill its owner.

Others speculated that he would keep it as it was, imprisoned and locked up just as people usually lock away painful memories. He would find another trade as a maintenance man somewhere.

Opinions differed as to the fate of the mill. The only thing that was agreed upon was that Sayeed would never resume work at the mill which had committed this deliberate crime against his father with malice and in cold blood.

Although most people in the village were upset at Abdul Mawla's death, their feelings and business interests were much more affected by the permanent stoppage of the windmill.

The women were particularly most affected because of the close bonds of affection they had formed for the windmill. This feeling started the very first day on which Abdul Mawla brought the mill. Previously they only know of the small hand-mills with the stone querns which they used at home. Each woman would get up almost at midnight and work till dawn operating the hand-mill. She would

39

place a piece of leather under the quern to collect the flour. Next to her, she would place a bowl filled with wheat or barley grains. She would sit on the floor, one leg extended before her, then lean over the quern and turn the stone with one hand, taking handfuls of grain with the other hand and pouring them into the opening of the quern. When her arm grew tired, she would change position and carry on in this manner. To dispel the loneliness of the night and to keep awake, she would sing old love songs, or war songs glorifying the victory of the village over its enemies in a battle which took place a long time ago. Or she might sing a modern song attacking the male sex. By morning, she would have completed the task until only a few grains remained in the bowl.

When the mill arrived at the village it was difficult for the women to believe that a machine was capable of grinding whole sacks of grain in the space of an hour. One of their oft-repeated expressions was: 'Oh, God, isn't this magic?'

This exclamation was repeated by every one of them whenever they sent out a quantity of grain to be turned into flour. They would pinch a small quantity of the flour between their fingers and feel its texture. As soon as they discovered that it was of the finest degree of smoothness, they would repeat those very same words to express their astonishment and delight. All the women in the village were unanimous in their amazement and admiration at the miracle which saved them from staying up half the night, saving them from exertion and misery ... struggling to stay awake with a few feeble songs. The fondness they carried in their hearts for the windmill soon became the topic of their songs at wedding parties.

So it was natural that when the mill met with this crisis in its life, the women would be affected most in the village.

The children spent the first day after the death of Abdul Mawla scribbling on the white walls the words of the obituary eulogy which Ma'touk bin Saadallah, the village poet, had composed in honour of the deceased. It listed his virtues stressing his services to the community by setting up the windmill. This established the village as the most prestigious one amongst all the other neighbouring villages. The older men spent that day musing over Sayeed's plans regarding the windmill.

Perhaps they could have gone and asked him outright what he intended to do, but they preferred to respect his feelings and watch events take their normal course, without disturbing Sayeed with their insensitive questions.

By the morning of the following day, just as some of the villagers were about to take the first sip of their morning tea, they were startled to hear the throbbing sound of the mill once more shattering the calm of the village, pulsating determinedly, resolute and purposefully! It was greeting them in its familiar usual words:

'Good morning!'

The first thing that crossed their minds was that Sayeed had sold the windmill to someone in the village, but who was that person amongst them who agreed to purchase a killer windmill?!

That question caused some of them to put down their cups of tea even before swallowing the first delicious sip, and hurry towards the windmill. Some of them left their homes carrying their cups with them and enquired in mouths full of bread: 'Who is he? Who bought the mill?'

The last thing they expected to see was Sayeed carrying out the running of the mill after his late father. Yet that was what happened. All those who arrived at the mill found Sayeed wrapping the sash with its many folds around his waist. He held the stick in his hand and took over his father's place.

They stood there dumbfounded, rubbing their eyes in amazement and disbelief. Some of them could not bear watching and ran back to the village, shouting at each person they came across:

'Sayeed! Sayeed! Sayeed! ... has taken over his father's place at the windmill!'

Even the children grasped the meaning and hurried home to inform their mothers. The mill was spouting its smoke high up into the air as if eager to join the soul of its departed former master. Its noise rose up over the murmurs of astonishment:

'Tick tick ... tick tick ... tick tick ...'

Its rhythm whirred on ... this time it definitely was like the sound of a galloping herd of horses, pounding the ground rapidly, powerfully and determinedly across mysterious and unknown paths.

Fasten Your Seat Belts

I was travelling for a rest ...
Sluggish clotted blood ran in my veins like swamp water ...
somewhere in this world I would find some rest and relaxation.
I was travelling for a rest ...
White plains stretched out as far as the eye could see, expansive
and undulating ... interspersed with blue lakes and white tents which
rose up in its low lands, while up above rose chains of snow-capped
mountains.
And I was travelling for a rest ...
I had booked my flight and stood on the boarding ramp waving
my handkerchief in farewell. I chose a seat by the window and
settled down ... what pleased me equally was that on the seat next to
mine sat a woman on her own. She was unaccompanied by either
husband or children ... a lone traveller like myself. I fastened my
safety belt and closed my eyes, dreaming of my beautiful
companion. The plane took off and I immersed myself in the clouds.
I was above the clouds. They changed shapes and colours,
constructed various worlds and destroyed them. I watched her. She
was looking all around the interior of the aeroplane. Her shoulders
were bare, delicious and tempting ... she had removed her jacket,
exposing a sleeveless blouse. Her face was dainty like that of a
child. She was most probably an American returning from visiting
relatives in Libya ... or perhaps she was a Swede, a German or an
English tourist. All this was beside the point. What mattered most to
me was that she was on her own, attractive and sitting next to me.
One slight movement and one little word from me and we could
open up a whole new world between us into which my blood could
flow and where I could find a cure for my malaise. I looked with
desire at her arm which flowed like a river of honey ... we were
separated by a short space, no more than a span.
I waited for her to start a conversation. It was my first trip abroad
and I had heard a lot about the boldness and daring of foreign
women. It was they who initiated the conversation. It was the lady
who stretched out her soft hand towards your curly hair, asking
permission to touch it and enjoy the feel of its texture. She was the
one who gazed at your dark complexion, tanned by the sun, and was

captivated by it. That's what I'd been told by people back home until I was persuaded to venture forth, book this flight and spend a holiday abroad.

I started to run my fingers through my hair in an effort to attract her attention to the fact that it was curly. I also coughed and cleared my throat, smiled an fidgeted in my seat to alert my lovely neighbour to the other fact, that my complexion was tanned by the sun. She remained determinedly aloof with her nose stuck up in the air. I was equally determined to overcome her obdurate pride. 'Just you wait, my little companion, I'm not such a stupid Bedouin as you might think! I know from which corner to nibble your tender shoulder!' I mused to myself.

I watched her arm, flowing softly, from her naked shoulder and decided to start my holiday in earnest!

I removed my jacket too. I moved a little closer to her seat. My shoulder inched its way to bridge the gap between us. I wanted to reach out to her and fasten on to her, to draw out the warmth of her fresh body and warm the cold blood in my veins. I was careful to make this move appear inadvertent, with no trace of stalking or prowling. To camouflage my intentions I lit a cigarette and drew a deep breath, then moved my shoulder in such a way that it seemed as if I was just making myself comfortable in my seat. I nearly reached my objective, but she deliberately fidgeted too and moved away to the far corner of her seat, as if allowing me to relax and take up as much room as I wanted.

She had now introduced a new distance between us ... which was more difficult to negotiate. It was easy to cover the first gap, but in order to bridge this new distance I had to forego all pretence at reasonable behaviour. Any new move on my part would be too obvious. I looked all around me and when I discovered that no one was watching I was encouraged to resume my creeping movements. The muscles on her arm quivered. Her skin had a rosy glow like the blush on a ripe peach and I was the cunning fox endeavouring to pounce on it and snatch it with my paws.

I leaned on the dividing arm between our seats. I had to muster all my courage and expertise and make my shoulder inch its way: innocuously, calmly, unhurriedly. She was gazing straight ahead, chewing one of the sweets which the stewardess had passed around earlier. That fixed frontal gaze of hers disconcerted me. I sensed that it was a false ploy designed to throw me off the scent and that she was fully aware of my wicked intentions. She paid them the fullest of attentions and her ears were alert to every creeping noise my shoulder made against the back of the seat. She sat there holding her ground ... whilst the nuisance of a distance between us still gaped open its jaws ...

Ahead of me still lay a difficult hurdle which I had to overcome. In the past I had travelled long journeys and covered extensive distances on foot. As a child I often accompanied my father as he went about his business to reap and sow. Yet this accursed distance of no more than a few inches which separated us seemed the most arduous journey I've had to undertake. I was determined to tackle it and quench the thirst of my shoulder upon her marble-like arm.

I stared straight ahead to make my actions seem unintentional and involuntary, as if my shoulder was moving of its own accord, independent of my will. This was not true of course, for all my will and determination were concentrated here, in this shoulder attempting to cover the short distance between us. For a fleeting moment, like the blinking of an eye, it appeared as if I had reached my target and that my arm had made contact with hers. It was about to cling to hers in an embrace which diffused all its yearning and longing, but I was foiled again. With an imperceptible movement which I failed to detect, my companion must have sensed the near proximity of my shoulder, for she shrunk even further into herself. I wasn't aware how this took place, all I knew was that a new distance, exceeding the latest one, had opened up yet again between us. All my efforts and patience had been in vain and I was overcome with a deep sorrow.

For an instant I decided to give up this childish game. It occurred to me that such attention was unseemly and unbecoming in a man of thirty. I had to give it up and retreat peacefully back to my seat. However, I discovered that my shoulder refused to budge, as if it had entrenched itself into a tactical position from which retreat would be impossible. I felt that if I failed to allow my shoulder to make contact with hers, take sustenance from it, I would experience such disappointment, besides which all others would seem insignificant.

Throughout my life I had met only with disappointment in my attempts to get acquainted with women. I used to drive around day and night through the streets of my city, like a frenzied stray dog seeking to satisfy the hunger of my emotions, only to retreat and drag my failure behind me day after day, night after night, the society of emotional and sexual repression, had denied me the chance to have any normal and healthy relationship with the opposite sex.

I viewed the distance with unbounded vexation. I shall struggle against it till death ... it was the last hurdle before winning my goal. She had shrunk into corner of her seat until there was no more space left, her body so tightly contracted that it was not possible for her to shrink any further. The siege was now secure, there was no more distance than the span of three fingers.

I waited a while until the stewardess passed by, her smile preceding her. I glanced furtively at my neighbour. She was still gazing straight ahead but signs of the siege were showing clearly on her face. Her nostrils were flared in anger, her eyebrows were knitted together. Irritation settled like fine dust over her features, but this had not affected her spirit. The distance still stood between us. I did not stop for a moment to consider my neighbour's feelings of annoyance, discomfort or tenseness. My shoulder was like a ravenous wolf, exposing its fangs, slinking warily towards its prey, creeping silently like the march of death's feet. My muscles were convulsed with fear as if terrified to plunge into this adventure only to encounter cruel defeat. I had to move at the same pace as the hours' hand on my watch, which showed the hour of five, then six, then seven without seeming to move at all. It moved imperceptibly like the earth which rotated daily without us feeling anything under our feet ... it was a sluggish slow motion.

Perhaps a long time elapsed before I was finally aware that the damned distance had been strangled and was dying. Indeed I nearly heard it scream as I muffled its breath with the slow advance of my shoulder. But just as I was about to attain my happiness and taste victory, it appeared as if the plane had suddenly expanded and the seat had moved away a few inches. This allowed my little neighbour to find another corner into which to squeeze and provide the opportunity for a new space to develop between us!

A heavy cloud of sorrow descended upon me, the gap was the same as the one which originally existed between us ... the nuisance of a distance was sticking its tongue out at me in mockery and derision! I realised that if I persisted in my efforts to reach her, I would have to lean bodily towards her which would make me look like a tilted vessel! It was impossible for me to do so without alerting another passenger to my game and to the fact that I was annoying this little lady. Despite this difficulty I refused to retreat. To do so now appeared to me nothing but failure and defeat. I had to go on. I could still see her naked tempting arm over which my shoulder salivated. I had to resume another battle, one which I waged with increased embarrassment. Beads of perspiration gathered on my forehead, but I was determined to cross the breach. My shoulder resumed its slow deliberate movement picking up signals, and acting as my observer. Expressions of annoyance covered her face, as if the thing that was moving towards her was the claws of some mythical creature emerging out of some concealed and mysterious cave to vanquish her!

I looked all around me ... everything was quiet. Some of the passengers were engaged in conversation, others had buried their heads in the clouds, some were reading papers. No one was aware of this battle being waged inside the aeroplane. The entire place was quiet, as if collaborating with me against my neighbour. This gave me confidence and charged my shoulder with new energy to resume its crawl. It was as if the aeroplane had shut down its engines and landed on the surface of the moon. The earth, stars and heavenly bodies had all discarded their solemnity and each spun joyously around their axis. My shoulder reached to hers at last and knelt on the marble of her arm. The pores of my skin were overwhelmed by a delicious shiver, which spread from my shoulder to my whole body. I felt my blood being freed from its cloying heaviness and run free like wild horses untouched by the hand of a trainer galloping across limitless wide plains. I sucked the nectar of pure happiness whose flavour my taste buds savoured. My ecstasy, however, was short lived. My companion seemed about to utter a scream loud enough to smash the hulk of the aeroplane, but I didn't know whether it was because of me or not ... I suddenly realised to my horror that someone was sitting behind us and without turning round I knew that he had watched the whole spectacle. I felt as if I had been ejected out of an open window of the aeroplane, to land on the ground in a smashed heap! My happiness vanished like the mist. I found myself break off in mid flight and shrank into the furthest corner of my seat. A great sense of shame and humiliation drenched my body with sweat, as if I was a child who had wet its underpants!

The absurdity and ugliness of what I had been doing suddenly hit me. I reproached and reprimanded myself because I had behaved like an uncouth and boorish person, unable to conduct himself with civility and act in good taste. I was like a stagnant pond exuding bad smells! It was within my ability to strike up an amiable conversation with my companion regarding the journey, the aeroplane or the clouds. She could have been friendly and we could have a pleasant conversation regarding the journey and where I was aiming for. Instead I had bothered her with my creeping shoulder. I felt all eyes in the aeroplane besiege me and cover my face with slimy spittle. I was a scared rat caught in a trap. With great difficulty, I made myself turn round and face the passenger sitting behind us in the hope that his presence was a figment of my imagination, spoiling my enjoyment. It was no delusion! He sat bolt upright in his seat with broad shoulders and bombarded me with his eyes! When our eyes met, he smiled mischievously and pointed with his finger at the instruction panel which was glowing with a red warning aimed at the passengers:

'FASTEN YOUR SAFETY BELTS'.

It seemed that we were passing over an air turbulence. I fastened my belt and turned my head to the clouds. They looked like the face of an old man, with a dark beard streaked with grey ... it was the face of a vigorous old man with an easy conscience who was looking at me with sadness in his eyes.

8

The Death of the Water Carrier

'Greetings. Have you heard?'
    'Greetings to you too. Nothing bad I hope?'
    'Old Mother Sayeeda ...'
'What's the matter with her?'
'The worst has happened ... Mother Sayeeda has gone and lost her mind this morning ...that's what's the matter with her!'
The news blasted through the village like a gust of wind. It travelled at the same magical speed with which all strange news usually did. People discovered in such titbits an exciting flavour lacking from their normal routine topics of conversation. Such subjects usually covered events like the birth of a mule, or the price of a kilo of wheat going up by three piastres. Or it revolved around the recollections of the old people who chewed their memories around in their toothless mouths as if to compensate for their inability to masticate food. Their reminiscences were usually about the war, and the past which – alas – could never be recaptured.
The news soon occupied the whole population of the village, old and young alike. Women spent long hours sitting by their ovens, savouring the warm blasts of air which emanated from them, inducing a soothing drowsing effect which contributed to prolonging the duration of such gatherings. The old men congregated in the courtyard of the mosque as was their habit. They would have been quite happy to do all their praying, eating and drinking there had it not been prohibited. The young men as usual were glued to the few rickety and faded chairs which added such a drab atmosphere to what stood for the only coffee shop in the village. All those people were united by the same topic of conversation, which was that Old Mother Sayeeda had gone crazy that morning. Even the children who usually were busy with make-believe games, inventing whole nations complete with generals and armies which warred against each other, forsook their play and raced towards the tumbledown dilapidated shack where Mother Sayeeda lived to observe her at close quarters.
Mother Sayeeda was an old woman of 50 with dark complexion. She earned her living by carrying water to the houses which had no plumbing installed. Her charge never varied, it was fixed at six

meleems for each load, no more or less.

Each person in the village claimed – without even having the decency to hang his head down – that he was the first to detect with his unusual perception, that something was wrong with her! They all saw how the old woman had refused that morning to carry water for anybody. When people came to enquire as to the reason for her refusal, she threw dirt in their faces and shouted at them that she was not their fathers' nor their grandfathers' servant and that they were all apes! Her son Mansour, the only man of breeding amongst them, would return that day or the next – she was certain of that – and prove his superiority over them all and show them that his mother was the most esteemed of mothers.

She carried on in this vein for a long time. The only thing that made sense to them all was that she was insane! Mansour, of whom she spoke, was her only son. He had left the village to join the army more than three years ago. In all that time he had never returned or communicated with his mother. Mother Sayeeda knew nothing of his whereabouts except that he had travelled with the army from Tripoli to Burga. She spared no efforts in trying to obtain some news about him. She even looked for a scribe and instructed him to write a letter on her behalf. In it she conveyed her longing, her reproach and her anxiety. She enquired as to his whereabouts and asked him how he could neglect his mother like this. She hoped everything was alright with him. She did not omit to ask the scribe to write for him a few lines of verse which she was inspired to compose, which started something like: 'Separation, dear heart, tastes bitter...'

She placed the letter inside an envelope with coloured edges which she bought from the shop of Haj Khalifa. She also bought a 1 1/2 piastre stamp and stuck that on the self-addressed envelope which she enclosed with her letter. She addressed the envelope with the only address she knew: her son's name, then 'a soldier in the Libyan army, Burga'. She posted the letter and tearfully awaited the reply. Month after month passed by but still no news arrived. Mother Sayeeda frequented the post office every week, standing by the small window in front of the counter where the post was distributed. The old man who ran the post office, with the expressionless face, read out the names of the recipients until all the letters were distributed. Then he locked the small window, still with an expressionless look on his wrinkled face.

Yet Mother Sayeeda would not give up. She remained standing by the small window for a little while longer, unable to believe that Mansour had failed to reply yet again. She would then drag her feet back to her rundown hut in tears ... the same tears often preceded her meandering steps when she was in that state. She would go back and knock on the closed shutters of the small window, which would then open. The impassive face of the postmaster would confront her and ask :

'Yes?'

'Tell me, please has my son Mansour sent a reply?'

'I've already told you, there is no letter for you. All the letters have been handed over there in front of your eyes! There's nothing for you ... nothing.' He would then shut the window in her face and mutter :

'Some people know no rest and can't leave those who are resting in peace ...'

She felt heartbroken and distractedly made her way back home ... tears preceding her as she shuffled and dragged her feet over the dusty earth.

The amazing news circulated around the village like a whirlwind anxious to terminate its journey and return to its source. People just refused to be convinced. Each of them would listen to the person who was giving assurances and swearing by all that was holy, repeating that Mother Sayeeda was indeed 'gone'. The other person would express his disbelief, then with the words of denial still fresh on his lips: 'No, no ... this is impossible! This is hard to believe, Mother Sayeeda is a sober and sensible woman. It's very unlikely that she is insane...' , would then go on his way and inform the first group of people he met:

'Greetings. Have you heard the news?'

'Greetings to you too. Nothing serious we trust?'

'Old Mother Sayeeda! She's gone crazy! This morning she's lost her mind!'

The new group would express their disbelief, whereupon his voice would rise up with indignation just like Mother Sayeeda herself, and he would assure them and swear oaths that the news was correct:

'I assure you, by God, that this is true! How could it be false when I saw her myself this very morning with my own eyes!'

Each one of them would then go on to relate the story, supported by oaths and swearing by all that was holy, that they had actually witnessed the event for themselves. In due course, the attitude of the whole population of the village changed towards Mother Sayeeda. They all started to regard her with a great deal of awe and reverence. She was no longer that poor helpless woman they used to curse and abuse when she was late in delivering their water. She acquired an aura of power and authority, she became an intimidating woman as if she was the possessor of some great secret. They feared her because of her power over the genie king and his underlings who were conscripted to serve her.

Many feet beat a track to the little hut where she lived, penitent and contrite, the same feet that used to kick her in the past. Many regrettable stupid actions had been committed against her. The many mouths which often spoke disdainfully of her, who uncharitably cursed and insulted her when the occasion demanded it, now kissed her hands in supplication, humility and respect.

Many of the old women in the village who used to despise her and hurt her feelings now began to realise the extent of the great wrongs they perpetuated against her. Each one of them filled censers with various kinds of incense. They sold a few eggs in order to afford buying some candles worthy of the status of Mother Sayeeda. Then they made their way to the shack where she lived, trailing their skirts and cloaks behind them, wept and kissed the ground at her feet as acts of atonement. They spent long hours begging forgiveness and beseeching her :

'Mercy, Mother Sayeeda ... we are helpless and our hands are tied behind our backs! Please bless us Mother Sayeeda. We beg your forgiveness, oh Mother Sayeeda ...'

Mother Sayeeda felt pity and compassion in the face of all these outpourings and she graciously murmured now and again :

'I forgive you!'

Some people brought along a sick son or a paralysed daughter, hoping for a miraculous recovery through a blessing from the pious occupant of the neglected hut. They implored and entreated:

'We beg you to use your influence and act as an intermediary with God, oh pious, honourable Mother Sayeeda!'

In spite of all the clamour and notoriety which the people set around Mother Sayeeda, she remained tranquil and composed. She rarely broke her silence or indulged in eccentric behaviour. When she did, her actions were regarded by the crowd as conduct sanctioned by God's various servants. She sometimes ate soil, or pulled her wild flyaway hair, at other times she cried and howled, calling for her absent son :

'Mansour, Mansour, Mansour...'

When such fits of sobbing and yelling were over, she would quieten down and start talking in a deep reproachful voice, as if her son was actually standing there in front of her, hot stinging tears brimming from her eyes:

'You have no right to treat me like this, you traitor! You keep away year after year, then come here today after this long absence as if nothing had happened! You never thought once of your mother, waiting anxiously for you! Never said to yourself that you have an old mother who might be worrying over you... never cared that your poor mother was suffering like this because of your unkindness. Are you satisfied with all this, you traitor? By God, son, your mother is angry with you!'

The same tears coursed down the furrows of her wrinkled anguished face. All this reinforced the unshakeable conviction in the minds of he assembled people that holy angels, who served her, had brought her son to her. He was invisible to their eyes. There she was addressing him and reprimanding him in words which only an abandoned mother would use. One of the old men in the village even went so far as to swear that he had actually seen the ghost of her son, Mansour, standing there in front of her, white and transparent like an angel.

It was the habit of the visitors to arrive at Mother Sayeeda's hut just before daybreak and remain there till nightfall. The next shift of visitors would then take over, with more requests for her blessing and asking her favours.

Things went on in this way until one morning when some children and old women made their way to Mother Sayeeda's place as usual. They discovered that the hut was deserted. Their mouths hung open and their eyebrows shot up in astonishment as they beat their breasts. They were surprised because Mother Sayeeda never left her hut, and if she did she never strayed far off. Yet here they were unable to find her at home or anywhere near it; not even in the nearby houses scattered around it.

After an extensive search in which the old and young participated, Mother Sayeeda was discovered lying sprawled on the sand outside the village. She was near her end and in her death rattle. They crowded all around her. She lifted her head up, its wild mantle of dishevelled hair was covered with sand and soil. She looked up at them out of demented eyes, framed with eyelashes covered with dust and sand. She gasped in a feverish whisper:

'Go away! Get away from me and leave me alone in peace ... my son Mansour is calling me ... my son, I'm coming to you ... make way for me to join my son ... Mansour is saying to me: "Oh, mother here I am." Mansour, my son ... Mansour ... Mansour!'

Tears, those same tears, washed over her ravaged face. The

nearby hills echoed the sad cry of Mother Sayeeda, as if sharing this mother's grief.

Far ... far off ... the wind carried away that anguished cry and dissipated it across the vast and empty land.

Mother Sayeeda gasped her last breath, repeating the name of her absent son whom she had not set eyes on for more than three years.

9

The Locusts

Just before nightfall a man came rushing into the village, spreading his cries throughout the place as if he was an alarm siren. His voice was charged with emotion, anguish and trepidation as he warned the people that a swarm of locusts was gathering just outside of the village. They were settling for the night on one of the nearby plains, about five kilometres away.

The inhabitants were immediately transformed into a collection of demented people, scurrying around hither and thither in consternation and alarm. It was obvious that every person in that village felt that a dreadful monster was stalking them round every corner, every bend and behind each tree trunk.

Some of the people went to their trees and crops and fastened their eyes upon them, looking at them with longing and regret. It was a certainty that at sunrise the following day the locusts would have reduced all that greenery and vegetation to mere memories.

Haj Salim stood at the top of his field surveying it with sorrow and anxiety, not even bothering to control the tears which glistened in his eyes. For once he didn't throw stones at the birds which alighted on it, nor did he shout in his hoarse voice as usual at the sheep approaching the field. It was obvious that the news of the locusts had a paralysing effect upon him.

There was no other talk in the village except of the locusts. The stories being related by the leaders of the village died on their lips. The women who gathered in clusters in the village square or stood by one of the wells to draw water, forgot in that instant to gossip about other women, giving their character assassination a rest. Nothing occupied them except this horrendous ghoul of locusts – this infestation which would commence at sunrise its destructive invasion of the their little village. The locusts would lay all trees in the vicinity bare, denuded of their verdant garments, depriving them of their luxurious foliage and transforming them into dry sticks. They would in all likelihood take the food out of the mouths of Haj Salim Mabrouk's family, Omran's children and every other person in the village. Their entire livelihood was invested in their trees and crops which were going to be reduced to just a trace in the blinking of an eye. The locusts were going to turn each verdant inch of their land into a barren wilderness. The locusts ... the locusts ... nothing but the locusts! A number of other incidents usually united the villagers and dominated their topics of conversation. These ranged from a death, an arrest by the police for a crime committed or when an elderly woman went mad. But no other incident monopolised their conversation, united their feelings and destinies, or manifested such terror in their eyes, and in every step they took, as this one. In all the village's long history, no other event affected them so deeply as the one which was about to take place. The reaction was evident in their faces and the manner of their speech.

As was the custom of the men in the village, whenever danger came knocking on their doors, they always felt the urge to congregate at the mosque. Now they all hastened there. The mosque was the focal point for the gathering of crowds. This happened on two occasions: whenever it was a feast day or whenever a danger threatened their village. The whole population stood hunched together as if speaking with a single voice. They sounded angry. Their faces were covered with anguish, they waved their hands, with their prominent blue veins, nervously into the air.

Some of the old men started to recount stories of the distant past, when locusts attacked their village, which was blossoming fresh, beautiful and verdant like a new bride turning into a barren land in which only the owls hooted. Two years passed by before the village was able to regain its vestments stripped by the locusts.

Another old man told an even more exaggerated story which he said happened a long time ago. About ten men were spending the night somewhere out on the plains. They were attacked by a swarm of locusts while they slept and by morning not a trace of them was ever found. 'Yes ... even the bones were gone! They consumed the bones as well, my friends!'

Al-Fagi Musbah took up the thread of the story and proceeded to talk in his own inimitable way about the locusts. He raised both hands high up above him, as if shielding himself against a thunderbolt from the sky. He opened his eyes wide with awe, as he always did whenever he invoked the names of the genies who were the friends of the genie king! His spittle flew around and his bushy white beard trembled as he went on talking. He claimed that when Almighty decides to put an end to the world, he would do so by means of a great plague of locusts. They would consume all the peoples of the earth also all the animals and plant life, demolishing whole palaces and maybe even steel and iron!

Horrendous stories about locusts and their dangers ... locusts ...

56

nothing but locusts! The men of the village stood there, anger displayed on their tanned faces, keenly feeling the tragedy of the situation. The stories told by the old men incensed them and filled their hearts with rage and hatred against the locusts. They felt that no other catastrophe on earth, not even death or the plague, could possibly equal the enormity of this one.

An old man was muttering, his whole being trembling because of the imminent disaster:

'Mercy, oh God! Forgive us, oh Lord!'

An angry voice rose up asking:

'What ideas have you come up with now?'

Other voices followed suit:

'Yes, men, what are we going to do?'

Voices sprang up everywhere, all of them asking questions. The air was filled with question marks, their tops hooked in perplexity: 'What are we going to do? What's the solution?'

The first suggestion came from Al-Fagi Musbah who said that the only thing to do was for all of the assembled company to hurry that night to the shrine of the Holy Master, Abu Kandeel. There must light candles and burn incense, then beg him to intervene with God in order to avert the danger. Afterwards they could all return to their homes and sleep in peace, because their Master Abu Kandeel would not let them down. He would soon divert the locusts away from the path of their village.

But soon Al-Fagi Musbah's suggestion was brushed aside in a flood of other ideas, amongst which was one from Omran. Everyone took him seriously because he was forty years of age – past the reckless age of youth which gave him distinction, and had not yet reached he age of senility, which was even more of an advantage. His solution was to build fires in separate locations of the village in the hope that the locusts would fly off because of the smoke, but there was no guarantee that this method would work. The villagers continued to crane their necks and strain their eyes awaiting further suggestions in spite of Omran who was angrily shaking his fist and head, defending his solution.

Al Mabrouk, meanwhile, hung his head in deep thought and said nothing, he fidgeted uncomfortably where he squatted. Mabrouk was twenty-five-years old, with a wide forehead, a slightly tanned complexion and his eyes were like two flames, above which rose sparse eyebrows. His father had died leaving him with a large family to support and a small field where he toiled daily. He barely managed to extract a meagre morsel of a livelihood for such a large

57

family. The idea that floated around in his head appeared ridiculous. He was afraid to voice it in case they all thought it was ludicrous and laughed at him. They might even begin to doubt his sanity. He was still thinking as he sat there in silence.

Someone nudged him and drew his attention to the fact that they were all waiting for his reaction to Haj Salim's idea. The latter wanted them to make preparations for frightening the advancing locusts away by beating on drums and tins, ringing bells and tinkling glass, thus creating as much noise and clamour as possible in order to drive the little beasts away. When everyone heard this suggestion, they ceased craning their necks and straining their eyes, looking for any more ideas. However, this solution appeared silly to Mabrouk. He looked around at their dust-stained faces, and they all seemed firm and resolute. His idea was no more ridiculous than the one proposed by Haj Salim. A tall farmer, with a long moustache asked him:

'Well, Mabrouk, speak up! What's the matter with you? It is not your habit to remain silent. Don't you like the Haj's idea? If not say so.'

Mabrouk replied:

'No. I don't think it's such a good idea!'

Everyone was most curious and surprised. Haj Salim, who proposed it, stayed silent listening attentively to what this young man had to say against his idea. Mabrouk then explained that if they succeeded in chasing away the locusts they would only head for another location. They would settle on other places where there were people, crops and where 'hearts throbbed'.

The Haj felt obliged to agree, but the tall farmer forestalled him and asked him with great perplexity:

'What are you trying to say Mabrouk? Do you want us to sign an agreement with the locusts when they arrive at our village that they would not annoy neighbouring villages "where there are people and crops and where hearts throb"?'

Haj Salim seized the opportunity to further justify his own suggestion :

'The thing that matters most of all to us is to save our land and crops. Mine seems the best idea proposed so far!'

Other voices added their agreement: 'Yes, that's the best idea we've heard so far.'

Mabrouk went on talking as if nobody had interrupted him:

'What do you say, brothers, to this idea ...'

The night was descending all around them. Their faces were

getting indistinguishable in the gloom. The evening breezes were blowing on them, fanning their faces. Some of them wrapped themselves closely in their cloaks. They craned their necks and listened attentively to Marbouk as he explained his idea. It was obvious that he felt a great conviction for it. His whole demeanour acquired the determined aura of a general explaining an intricate battle manoeuvre to his troops:

'My idea is this ... let us eat the locusts instead of them eating us!'

The group of people exchanged puzzled looks amidst the gathering darkness.

Someone voiced their incomprehension:

'What do you mean by "eating" them?'

Comprehension began to dawn on them slowly. They had all sometimes caught a few stray locusts as children and eaten them, but tackling unlimited columns of them was another matter. Perhaps what Mabrouk had said was odd, but it was no match to the strange silence that descended over the whole assembly as they listened to him carefully. Mabrouk carried on, clarifying his idea. A lot of the men could not help but suck at their lips and exchange dubious looks. Others curled their lips up in sneers as he outlined his plan. Every one of them should proceed that same night exactly before dawn towards the southern end of the village. Each of them must be sure and bring along an empty sack. Before them lay a battle such as had never been encountered before, a battle in which the only weapons employed were empty sacks. The locusts slept at night and were only awakened when touched by the warming rays of the sun. The villagers were to go to the place where they rested and proceed to pick them up and deposit them into the empty sacks. Afterwards they could return to the village and cook the locusts in their blackened cooking pots, thus transferring them from the insides of the sacks to their own insides! This would be the most distinguished battle of extermination in the history of locusts!

No sooner had Al Mabrouk finished explaining all this, than sarcastic remarks rose up everywhere from the crowd:

'An army led by a queen ...' some murmured mockingly.

Al-Fagi Musbah seized this opportunity to remind the group of his initial suggestion, urging them to hasten to the tomb of Sayidi Abu Kendeel, patron of all believers and the righteous.

Darkness was getting denser. Many children arrived to call their fathers home:

'Mother says supper is getting cold!'

59

Al-Mabrouk felt that they had not given his idea enough thought
and waited for the hubbub to die down before attempting to
convince them further :

'Listen, brothers ...'

He was trying to be heard when a voice rose up:

'In my opinion, what Al-Mabrouk says makes sense!'

'But this is an army! When they swarm they cover the face of the
sky! Yet Al-Mabrouk wants us gathered here, no more than fifty
men, to gather and dispose of them. This is impossible!'

Sheikh Mas'oud lifted his head up from deep contemplation and
said:

'Why only fifty of us? Why not the entire village, old and young,
women and children too? Let us collaborate in this operation.'

Silence reigned. Sheikh Mas'oud had added a new perspective to
the plan. It was obvious that they were all reviewing Al Mabrouk's
suggestion.

'I, too, agree that Al-Mabrouk's idea has a lot to offer.'

Soon others voiced their agreements.

'By God! Why don't we give it a try tonight? If this fails we'll
resort to Haj Salim's idea at daybreak.'

'We can kill two birds with one stone. We can destroy the locusts
on the one hand, and secure some food for our children for a few
days on the other hand!'

Only one person objected and still resisted this insane solution:

'You're all crazy! You're definitely all mad!'

Al-Fagi Musbah thumped the ground with his stick and departed
angrily. He was obviously incensed that the assembly had turned
down his suggestion in favour of an upstart, a lunatic idea from an
immature young man.

The crowd dispersed.

Early at dawn as cocks crowed and dogs barked at the stars and as
the howling of a wolf was carried across from a far-off place.
Exactly at that hour the south side of the village witnessed a
spectacle it had never seen before in its history. The crowd was
numerous. Ashour voiced the thought that was going on
simultaneously in each of their minds when he exclaimed :

'I never imagined the village held so many people!'

The one thing that united them all was the empty sack carried on
each shoulder. Apart from this they were an odd collection of men,
women, old people with bent backs, and children who were
prevented by either darkness or the cold from running around
everywhere.

One of the women even brought her suckling infant along. Amer arrived astride his donkey. Abdul Nabi brought with him a small hand-drawn cart which contained two or three sacks. A number of dogs ran in the wake of the crowd, dragging their tails behind them. The sound of the advancing people mingled with the barking of the dogs, the braying of the donkey and the squawking noises emitted by the hand-cart. The sound of trampling feet could be heard across the wide expanse of the plains.

Although spring was fast approaching, the breeze at this hour of dawn was cold and nippy. It stung their faces and swelled up their ears and noses. It was laden with the scent of the fruit trees and the crops. Each one of the people was able to distinguish the aroma of the orange blossoms in his orchard, the smell of the tender ears of corn in his field, or the dates on his palm trees. Their path was not illuminated by moonlight, but the stars which glittered like the eyes of heavenly creatures, dispelled some of the gloom.

When they reached the place where the locusts slept, shafts of dawn bursting forth across the horizon gave them enough light to see by, facilitating the task of picking up the locusts. Pink horns tinged with blue emanated from the red outline of the sky like flames, then blended in to the darkness until they melted away. The horns throbbed and shimmered with vitality, as if a mighty fire was blazing behind the horizon, glowing and radiating.

The locusts had chosen a wide empty plain over which to spread out. They appeared in the light of dawn like an endless row of golden ears of corn, ripe and ready for harvesting. This was the signal for the battle to commence ...

The people began to prepare themselves. The men took off their cloaks and placed them in separate heaps on the ground. They tied belts around their waists. They pulled their sleeves up, exposing brown forearms on which dark hairs sprouted. Those who wore wide pantaloons, pulled the legs up over their knees. The mother with the suckling infant chose a safe resting place for it under a tree. She kissed him and carefully wrapped him up in his shawl.

Amer tethered the two front legs of his donkey together and left him to munch grass. Some had brought water gourds with them. Some women carried small sacks containing loaves of bread, which they brought along as a precaution in case the children cried with hunger, and placed them in different locations.

The crowd did not wander about in different directions. They started simultaneously from the lower half of the plain, planning to move up gradually to the higher ground. All along the length of the plain advanced a straight line of people as if of one mind and one purpose. They all knelt upon the ground. Many fingers stretched out, large and small, rough and smooth, collecting locusts into the gaping mouths of the sacks. The extermination operation which was destined to take place that morning at dawn had commenced in earnest. Everybody was engrossed energetically in his or her task with unflagging determination. They were undeterred by the thorns or the sharp stones which cut their fingers, nor by any other insects which lurked in the undergrowth; even these were picked up with the same unfailing enthusiasm. All that mattered to them was to pick the locusts up as quickly as possible before the sun overtook them.

Some of the children started to run ahead of the advancing line of grown-ups, but they soon retreated in alarm following sharp cries of reprimand and restraint. Old Mother Sayeeda did not stop calling out that they must find the queen of the swarm before anything else. People started to sing in different parts of this lengthy human chain.

Some sang harvesting songs. The older men's voices rang out with jingoistic war songs from the days of the war against the Italians, for there was something of a similarity between the war and what they were embarked upon at present. They chanted :

'We are fighting the enemy amongst us ...
Our boys are brave ...our boys ...'

Another group sang out in harmony:

'Oh moon high above, high above
Wandering in the sky in the sky ...'

Even the children who went to the school of the village discovered how enjoyable it was to sing at this hour of dawn, in this wide open space. Soon their little voices filled the air with the national anthem.

As for the very young children not of school age yet, and who had not yet been taught any songs, they discovered that an echo lurking somewhere in the nearby hills and knolls, was answering back the pleasant sounds. They strained their ears and opened their little dark eyes wide in surprise and cried out in unison:

'Hoa! Hoa! Hoa!'

Which the echo instantly repeated: 'Hoa! Hoa! Hoa!'

They looked at each other in astonishment, then giggled and clapped their hands in unrestrained delight as if they had just stumbled upon the greatest discovery in the world.

Meanwhile, the locusts lay silent and still, as if they were dead.

The human column advanced steadily, sometimes it appeared broken, sometimes crooked. At other times it was a dead straight line in front of which the locusts seemed like wide expansive carpet being rolled up.

Each of them wished he could expand the spot allocated to him a bit further, so that he could gather as large a number of locusts as possible. When the gnarled hand of an old farmer moved towards the spot allocated to Omran, a quarrel would have ensued, had not the old man withdrawn his hand in the nick of time. It was because some of these old folk had been victims of the locusts in the past and bore a long-standing grudge against them, which drove them to shovel them up greedily, eagerly and savagely. They also felt joy in their hearts because they were able at last to take revenge for all wrongs committed against them by these insects.

Several voices rose up now and again urging the crowd to greater effort. One of the most vociferous belonged to Sheikh Mas'oud who kept shouting:

'Make haste, you men ... Take heart, you men ...'

He kept addressing the men although the dawn was witness to the fact that the long human column consisted of women and children too. His voice was echoed back across the valley and plains, as if they too approved of the undertaking.

In one part of the line, some seven or so people, amongst whom was Ashour, were so fired with enthusiasm that they decided to run a race. The first one to reach the high ground would win the wager. Although they were already quite exhausted, with beads of perspiration glistening on their brows despite the cold morning air, they ran with boundless energy. The others were gaining, but Ashour soon overtook them and outstripped them easily. He reached the finishing line way ahead and won the race. He stood at the top of the bluff, lifted both arms high up into the air jubilantly and shouted out his victory. It was plain to see that his feelings at that moment were like those of a great general who had won a most arduous battle.

The others soon caught up with him, their sacks bulging with locusts.

Just before full sunrise, the last person in the crowd had completed his task. They all stood up in disbelief, surveying the miracle they had just accomplished with their own hands. Each of them felt a great sense of pride as they smiled with pleasure and satisfaction. The earth of the plain was red. Only a handful of locusts which previously covered it remained, hopping around and these were soon chased by some children. Haj Salim was watching the red earth, repeating over and over again how even now he still could not believe that all this was possible. The women couldn't wait to return home so they could start fires and cook the locusts in large pots. They muttered incantations as each batch was completed. This would give them a break from the insistent pestering of their children, asking for more bread to eat. Many loaves were usually baked, but these were soon exhausted. The children would now discover that locusts tasted delicious. Their school bags which they tied with string and slung over their shoulders, and which normally contained only chunks of bread, would now be filled to capacity with cooked locusts.

The villagers returned home, carrying the full sacks on their backs. The happiness which filled their hearts was manifested on their faces. Even their steps appeared lighter as if they were dancing on air!

Abdul Nabi pushed his hand-cart along, crammed with three sacks bursting with locusts. He chased the children with it as if it was a car, shouting : 'beep ... beep ...beep' like a horn. The children scattered away from it, screaming in glee.

Ashour's donkey ambled on as if it, too, was happy. Even the cries of the baby carried on its mother's arm, sounded almost as lovely as a song. Ashour was still teasing and taunting the others who lost the race.

All of them seemed to have just discovered the bond that tied them together, thrilled at the discovery of feeling deeply fond of the village ahead of them, which appeared full of greenery as it was bathed in the morning sunlight. The sun was rising steadily and causing shadows to grow longer and longer as if they were those of giants. Sometimes the shadows mingled together into one huge long one which advanced forward as if it was the shadow of one person, one gigantic person, which the world had never seen mightier or taller.

10

The Sea has Run Dry

'Toot … toot … toot!'
The ship undocked and blew its whistle.
'Toot … toot!'
The sound wavered … grew short, then long … it was a farewell, handkerchiefs waving in the air of Naples. The sound of the ship's whistle aroused sadness in hearts, not a dark oppressive kind of sadness but a light pleasant sensation like a white cloud, that delicious sadness which accompanies moments of travel, farewell and waving of handkerchiefs in the air .. the ship sailed on.

Many sea gulls flew in its wake and all around it, screeched and spread their wings as they happily followed the ship on its journey on the tide. The ship ceased its farewell calls.

Naples receded in to the distance, then disappeared. The ship cut a path across the waves, raising a multitude of bubbles and white froth.

Naples was reduced that night to a pinpoint of light. All the shores of Italy appeared like thin strips of light, fading away until completely extinguished. Nothing was left but the night with its darkness, and the sea with its spray and waves. The span of the sky was spread out, sprinkled with stars and a yellow moon. The sea, under the stars, lay calm and gleaming, subdued and peaceful.

The ship glided over the waves, lightly and gracefully, pleased with the night, the sea and the stars. She was even happy with the various fishes which even now were swimming playfully around its hull, bumping against it and attempting to nibble it.

The ship was crammed with happy travellers. They dispersed around in the lounge cabin which was clean with comfortable chairs. The coloured lights were subdued and were reflected on the polished gleaming floor and the rows of glasses carefully stacked in tiers on wooden shelves behind the bar.

Old women sipped their coffees and chatted loudly. The men were playing dominoes and exhaling cigarette smoke. Introductions were made, and enquiries took place as to where everyone came from and where they were going. Passengers soon became friends, passing cigarettes around and exchanging addresses. Shoulders were slapped amiably. They thanked the Turkish waiter. Several children played around, jumping over the empty seats with their small shoes, or clung to the knees of the men and women.

The passengers were a hotchpotch of various nationalities, like those of any other ship. This collection included some Germans, Turks returning to Istanbul and Greeks returning to Piraeus and Athens. He was the only Arab journalist travelling alone. It was there they met. She was a young woman who gave the impression of a butterfly ancestry ... he was a young man who inspired those who met him with the impression that he would grow up into a distinguished old man.

She was wearing blue trousers and a short-sleeved blouse. He was dressed in a full suit with a grey neck-tie. Her blouse was multi-coloured. It had pictures of flowers, whales, the heads of gazelles interwoven with green, brown and mauve stripes printed all over it, exactly like the colour patterns on a butterfly's wings. Her complexion was tanned and her eyes were black, like the colour of black olives. One could tell from his features that he was an Arab. Her hair was black and done up in a pony tail, a headstrong spirited pony whose tail twitched and danced about constantly. He remained discreet aboard the ship. When asked what he was writing and about whom, he replied that it was a trade secret. She walked about gracefully. She didn't merely walk, she was a butterfly flitting around and alighting here and there.

He sat by himself on a large armchair by the window, a small black pipe always sticking out to the side of his mouth, holding a lighted match in his fingers. She played on the piano with well-trimmed fingernails. Her pointed heels made a tapping sound on the deck, just as her fluttering butterfly eyelashes tapped on the hearts of all men. He smoked his pipe, blowing thick clouds of smoke all around him, like a transparent screen which perpetuated the aura of mystery around him. She was a Greek returning to Athens after a tour of Europe. He was a writer, and like all Arab authors, had to earn his living through journalism. He was a prolific writer who had created many fictitious heroines whom he had never known. He endowed them with grace, elegance and beauty. Now, for the first time, he discovered a real-life heroine like the inventions of his imagination, soft, delicate and sweet.

Ever since the first night when he had seen her through his smoke screen, he remained watching her and listening to her from afar. As if he had discovered an unknown island in the middle of the ocean, he remained standing on its shores in order to savour the pleasure of the discovery. He made up his mind that the date of the invasion would commence the following day.

'Tomorrow!'

Tomorrow he would talk to her and get to know her. People aboard ships became friendly quickly and easily. He would ask her her name and exchange addresses with her. He would tell her about his stories and would be pleased to listen to the details of her journey and her life. She would undoubtedly tell him about her home in Athens and her studies. Conversation between them would cover several subjects until it reached the topic of 'woman, man and love between them'. He began to practise being a skilful navigator in the art of conversation steering the helm and at the appropriate moment bringing it to the subject of love. However, the next day dashed the hopes of the aspiring knight. He had assumed that like him, she spoke English, whereas she only spoke Greek. He puffed out thick clouds of smoke as he stood on deck, thumping a regular and violent rhythm on the ships' rail with clenched fists, as if it alone was responsible for the difference in their languages.

Why did all these different languages rise up like walls between people? We all laugh, rejoice, feel sorrow and love in the same language. Why couldn't we all communicate in a universal tongue? He wanted to tell her so many things and wanted to know so much about her, but the difference in their languages was a barrier between them preventing him from fulfilling his wishes.

He felt disappointment. His eyes and face expressed his sorrow. He returned to his chair and puffed black smoke out of his pipe in rapid and thick clouds, as if sending out smoke signals in a language no one could fail to understand:

'I'm depressed, frustrated and dejected!'

She sat down on a chair opposite him and looked at him. She didn't aim her gaze directly at him, but seemed to be looking at the curtains drawn over a porthole behind him. Yet this one indirect look worked wonders upon him. In one instant he forgot all his depression and unhappiness, it swept them away and threw them overboard. She returned to look at him more directly. They kept exchanging looks. She was obviously interested in him.

Like him she was intrigued. This exchange took place most probably because all the other passengers were middle-aged. The women were either wives, mothers or grandmothers. It was natural that they should be drawn together, not only because of the similarity in their ages, but because she was close to his heart and his highly-attuned emotions.

They resumed exchanging looks ...

They were communicating in a language different to all others in the world, it was the language of the eyes. He told her with his eyes: 'Where have you been all my life?' You are a creature of my imagination. I have agonised over your creation. I have spent many sleepless nights trying to weave out of your dress the wings of a butterfly, and convert the tapping sound of your heels into a tune strummed on a guitar!'

In the main cabin was a grey piano. The carpets were Turkish. The curtains over the portholes were green, half drawn and tied in the middle. The sea stretched behind them, blue and undulating. She played the piano expertly and skilfully, her fingers with the trimmed nails, moving adroitly over the keys. The tunes which emerged from it were like butterflies ... like little birds enfolded by wings tinged with many hues. She was talking to him in the language of music. She was sending out messages to him on the piano like the tapping of a Morse Code; transmitted via cables from ships, sea ports and high communication towers. The taps were short and light, but carried a multitude of meanings, as if informing him with their cipher: 'You're mine!' Far off the sea was embracing the sky.

He was known in his country as a revolutionary. He criticised everything. He wanted his city to be a perfect place, not only his own city but his own country. In fact he wanted the whole world to be a better place. Now in this place he felt a deep and firm conviction that he was existing in the midst of the world he dreamt of, reflected in the eyes of this descendant of Plato, the philosopher, who dreamt of the first Utopia. That evening he stood on deck. She joined him and rested her arms on the rail some distance away from him.

She was watching the sunset. He watched the large sphere of the sun, red and glowing like a luminous meteor spreading out its rays. The outline of the horizon shimmered with transparent glimmering hues. She stood like a worshipper. The small clouds interspersed around it, moved closer, surrounded the sun. The large disc was dextrously and nimbly evading their nets. He watched the duel excitedly and enthusiastically, rooting for the sun. Perhaps she felt the same. He nearly clapped his hands with delight every time the sun slipped away from the clutches of the nets and cried out:

'Oh, goal!'

The red glow of the sun was reflected on the waters of the sea as if some lamps were infused in its depths, illuminating it with radiance. The ship continued to glide. The various sea birds cried and screeched, tumbled and dived around in the air. The freshly painted hull of the ship reflected the golden glow which in turn was reflected in the waters of the sea. It surrounded the ship which appeared to be sailing on a halo of glowing light. The ship slid forward ...trailing behind it a long ribbon of horizon, brimming with lights, colours and scents ... but the horizon was never far off ... it was always the same distance away from the ship. The ship sailed on, horizon always at the same distance, as if tied to it by slack ropes trailing under the water, which continuously towed it along complete with its sun, its little clouds and glowing ribbon.

The sea was a carpet folded and rolled up by the ship. The earth was a sphere. The sphere rotated, thus preventing the sea water from pouring out. It also prevented people and cities from tumbling about and falling off the face of the earth. He wondered what would happen if the world stopped rotating for just one instant. What if a minor malfunction occurred in the mechanism, which caused a stoppage. The sea water would pour out into the atmosphere. Their ship would tumble out into the void. It would turn into a space ship floating away in the galaxy on an eternal journey with no ports of call, no ropes tying it to the quayside. It would sail forever with no need for fuel or provisions. There would not be any ports of Piraeus or Istanbul. It would be a ship with no ports, sailing on a universal ocean with no shores, no water, no limits and no bottom.

When this space ship made its sad farewells: 'Toot ... toot ... toot!' it would sound even more musical and expressive because it would be bidding farewell to an old world, in which people live, separated by walls of languages, religions, races and colours; until it disintegrates and falls apart. It would then welcome a new world, another spacious hospitable eternal existence.

She was his ideal world and she would accompany him on this journey into space. She would be the new Eve and he would be the new Adam. Together they would produce a new race of human beings with one colour, one religion and all speaking one tongue.

He looked at her with pleasure and asked himself naively:

'I wonder if she is indulging in the same fantasies?'

She was still at her place by the rails, watching the glow of the sun reflected on her face and her hair. She appeared like a being from another planet, who descended on the ship, still preserving the halo of light all around her. The ship sailed on, pulling the horizon behind it like a docile lamb. The world looked like a radiant globe. The sea gulls still screeched, playfully caressing the wind with their wings. A grey-coloured bird flew nearby and alighted on the rails close to her. Her eyes twinkled with a child-like pleasure. She moved forward, holding out her hand to catch it. The bird jumped off, she moved after it and they continued in this fashion until the bird stood quite close to him. She moved forward lightly, stretching out her hand but she didn't quite manage to catch the bird. She was now standing very close to him, their arms and bodies touched. Their fingers met and his were burning from the warmth transmitted by his shoulder which was pressed against hers. He too moved his hand towards the bird, it was an innocent unintentional moment of contact. He was able to grab hold of the bird, she drew a long sigh of relief and satisfaction. Her breath fanned his face. He handed her the bird and she moved away, while he trembled with delight.

He was overcome with a delicious sensation of pleasure. His breath was rapid as he thought to himself: 'I have just grasped a moment of happiness!'

The bird struggled in her grip. It shook its body, ruffled its feathers and flapped its wings, pecking at her hand angrily. What brought such a small bird here? Perhaps it was hoping to catch a little fish, but the hunter had become the hunted! What a tame but unfortunate hunter that little bird turned out to be!

The bird eventually managed to escape her clutches. He tried to recapture it for her, but it flew away. They followed its flight with their eyes as it spread out its wings and flew into the distance. He tried to tell her through sign language, using his lips and hands, that the bird was flying off to join its mate which waited for him on some distant shore.

She laughed although it was obvious that she did not understand what he was trying to say. He resumed looking into the distance. The large red disc was poised right over the edge of the sea as if preparing to dive. They both looked upon it as their property and were reluctant to lose it!

Just before it began to set, the sun looked like large ball resting over the surface of the sea. He imagined what it would be like if the sea were dry. He could have run towards the pretty ball and dribbled it with his feet, until he kicked it near her. They could then have had a friendly game of football.

He wished that the golden globe would remain in that position and never submerge, but it began to gradually dip into the briny water. Its lower edge began to submerge. He considered this better than nothing, but then half the disc began to dip in, whilst the top half remained there, radiating all over the sea. He begged God to keep the top half afloat, but this too began to disappear until only a tiny portion remained, like an ember glowing in the distance.

Eventually even that was gone. The sun had withdrawn its glowing mantle away from the world, which it loaned it for a short while. He looked at her.

Her eyes reflected the same anxiety. They exchanged looks as if telling each other in that other shared language which exceeds the narrow boundaries of ordinary ones:

'Our golden disc is lost!'

The magic aura which throbbed all around them disappeared quite suddenly, to be replaced by a gloomy melancholy seeping into every corner.

Later on they spent part of the evening in the main cabin with the rest of the passengers. As he exchanged looks with her, he felt that there existed between them a large depository of shared memories : the space ship, the tame hunting bird and the golden globe, sucked away by the horizon.

In her eyes he perceived the same sentiments!

The next day the shores of Greece appeared like a thin strip of horizon. When the ship docked at the port of Piraeus, when it blew its whistle in greeting, when ropes were thrown over the side to secure the ship to the quayside, he was still immersed in his happiness, unable to believe that she would disembark soon and that he would never see her again, or look into her dark eyes which were like the colour of black olives.

'Toot ... toot ... toot!'

The ship unfurled its handkerchiefs and waved them in farewell at Piraeus. This time the ship's whistle left a dark melancholy sadness in his heart. He went to the main cabin and looked all over for her, refusing to believe that she was no longer aboard, and that she was now on her country's soil. When he failed to find her anywhere the truth began to sink in. His favourite butterfly had flown off and her dark eyes had disappeared from his sight forever. In that instant he felt his Utopia disintegrate. The gentle butterfly possessed talons which snatched his happy dream world away. It left him as an unlucky bird existing in a world full of ruin, everything around him crumbled and fell apart.

There was something wrong even with the ship itself. It was no longer able to float easily as if suffering from sea sickness. The same sea sickness spread all over his body, his throat and all the cells of his brain. Everything swam and spun around: the world, the ship and his head. For the first time he was aware that the ship was full of old people. They sipped their teas or coffees rudely and ungraciously making loud slurping noises. The tables in the main cabin were

71

covered with cigarette burn marks like festering wounds. The fingernails of the waiter were long and dirty. An old Turkish mother insisted on hanging her washing on lines spread all over the ship.

He grew irritated with the main cabin and went up on deck to stand by his favourite spot near the rails. He felt desolate. The world was a rotating ball, his head spun and whirled. The sad thoughts which raced around his head felt sticky and woozy. The door knob of his cabin felt soft and sticky, the sea out of the porthole looked slimy, even the bunk bed was sticky when he threw himself upon it.

The whole world was a ball, a soft malleable ball. A bitter taste filled his mouth and the ship seemed tilted at a strange angle, as if it wasn't moving at all. It stood there poised, suspended in a strange unusual position. The sea had run dry. There existed a frightening ugly monster with huge whiskers, whose wispy ends ran with spittle. The monster's hairs were like large thorns, and it started sucking out all the waters of the sea. The sea was dry and the ship was floundering at the sludgy bottom, clumsily and hopelessly struggling futilely. It lay helplessly trapped in the slimy mire while out of his eyes ran sticky and despairing tears!